Happy Reading!

For additional information go to
http://authorklbrown.blogspot.com/

Heiress

By K.L. Brown

A special thank you
to those who have
helped make this book
possible.
Kimberly, Sam,
Jessica, Carol and Bradly.
Heiress wouldn't have
been possible without you.

Chapter One

Artois, early summer 1256

Jocelyn looked out from her perch on the battlements, absently gazing down at the vacant yard below her.

She should feel relief with the thought of her irksome company pressing on to leave her in peace at last. She was weary of being the center of attention, of finding the will to carry on a conversation with a stranger and pretend she was pleased to do so.

Her life had been nothing like she imagined it would be since she took hold of her inheritance, and she was growing more frustrated by the day.

Alas, her thoughts shifted from the yard below her and the group passing through her gates to a time in the not so distant past that molded her into the woman she'd become.

Jocelyn allowed her mind to wander to the hushed darkness where the fragments of dreams and reality collide until she was vividly reliving a tender memory of her past.

* * * *

She rode beside her aunt Suri and her two cousins, entering the battle in the wake of her uncle's men.

There was nothing left to fear for once the enemy saw the refreshed numbers of their foe advancing, they retreated, running for their lives.

Jocelyn's eyes beheld a man lying upon the ground in the distance. Her heart knew him at once for he had been a part of her soul for longer than she would ever care to admit.

"Bart!" Jocelyn cried, bringing her mount to a rearing halt. "Oh…nay!"

Jocelyn dismounted and was running across the trampled battlefield before her kinswomen could see what alarmed her.

Bart was lying on the ground at the base of a tree, his sword resting across his lap, his hands limp at his side.

Jocelyn knelt beside him, tenderly lifting his head to rest it on her lap.

His once sun-kissed complexion was terribly pale, his eyes searching her face, causing her to feel for a moment as though he didn't know her.

How could he not, they had all but grown up together.

"It should have been Jocelyn whom he loved," her cousin, Meredith, whispered to no one in particular, as she sat upon her mount in the distance.

Meredith's heart was breaking as she watched Jocelyn weep over the loss of the man she had loved for the majority of her life.

It was not right for Bart to be so blind to Jocelyn's devotion. Jocelyn would have given anything to have Bart look to her with love in his eyes.

Meredith dismounted and followed her cousin's footsteps to the base of the tree, kneeling beside Jocelyn to offer her comfort as best she could.

Jocelyn swallowed hard when Meredith joined her, wishing they could go back and change what had been done.

Bart had asked for Meredith's hand only days before, he'd sworn he loved her cousin as Jocelyn stood by, her heart aching for Bart to speak those very words to her.

Jocelyn would have accepted his offer in an instant, where Meredith could only stand in shock; her heart already lost to another.

"Meredith—" Bart whispered, bringing Meredith's attention to his strained countenance.

His eyes were dim and clouded over with pain, his hand gripping Jocelyn's so fiercely her fingers were swiftly turning white.

"Aye," Meredith answered, her voice heavy with sorrow.

"Give Cody my gratitude…tell him I am honored to call him my friend," Bart instructed, needing the man to know that after everything, he was grateful to him.

It was Cody whom Meredith had given her heart, it was Cody who freed Bart from his foe, allowing him to live and die with honor.

"I will," Meredith promised, giving way to her tears, allowing them to flow freely down her wind-burnt cheeks.

The man then looked up to the woman who was bending over him, her eyes filled with tears, her usual cheery complexion marred by her sorrow.

"Forgive me—" Bart whispered. "I fear it has taken death…for me to truly see you…you might have been more to me than a dear friend."

Jocelyn shook her head at his words, not willing to hear this, not now that he was doomed to leave her.

Bart's confession that he might have loved her would rip her apart; she could not bear to hear him speak such things to her, not when he lay dying in her arms.

Too overcome to speak, Jocelyn bent over him as his eyes closed, the life he once so vibrantly lived stilled, leaving him empty and lifeless in the arms of the woman who loved him.

* * * *

Jocelyn let out her breath in a mighty puff and shook her head at the distant horizon.

It was only two years ago that Bart was taken from her, and yet to think of that night brought fresh agony.

Even so, she could not keep the memory of it far from her thoughts. Ever was the image of that day there to haunt and bring her sorrow.

"Truly, Jo, was it so horrible?" Tomas asked from his place beside her on the battlements.

He was looking to the horizon, as she was; watching the large party of their most recent guests fade from sight.

"It was not you who was forced to entertain them," she answered, shaking her head a second time. "You sat back in your leisure, watching while I did my best to entertain and act kindly to those I would never have given entrance to my home at all."

Tomas was a good few years her senior and the captain of her father's guard. In his youth, he was her father's squire and was now on loan to her until she could manage to find a captain of her own.

As it was, she trusted Tomas and until her father complained about his absence she would keep him in her service.

"Aye, are you alright?" Tomas asked, obviously concerned about her well-being.

"Well enough," Jocelyn answered with another heavy sigh.

"Is that not the third party you have entertained this season, it is not yet mid-summer?" he questioned, reaching his hands out to rest them on the rough parapet, his pale blue eyes squinting at the distance.

"Aye," she muttered, unable to forget how she'd been passing her days.

Jocelyn forced herself to suppress her rising irritation with her peculiar situation and focus instead on the time when it would be her family coming to stay within the walls of her keep, and not some fool stranger seeking her hand in marriage.

She'd been mistress of Artois for a little less than two years and already she was being sought after by a throng of suitors she had no desire to entertain.

She was not yet ready to wed.

She was only just feeling that her heart might be on the mend, why must she jump into a marriage?

Jocelyn longed for love. She knew a good deal of woman her age were already married and had families of their own. She wanted this as well, but she was not about to give her heart to the first beggar that came knocking.

"I hate to be the one to spoil your most deserved respite," Tomas sighed, his rich voice breaking the silence. "It would seem you will find no peace after all, a party approaches."

He extended his hand, pointing to where a group of riders were materializing in the distance.

Tomas as well was growing weary of the constant stream of visitors that persisted on swarming Artois. It was past time the place was given a rest from entertaining strangers.

Jocelyn felt her resolve crumble, she wanted time to herself, to walk in the gardens, fly her hawk or hunt. She was tired of guests for the whole of one lifetime.

"Is it too late to make a run for it?" Jocelyn asked, knowing the answer to her own question, even as she knew her duty to those seeking her hospitality.

She had every right to turn any visitor away, but even so, to do so would be at the risk of offence.

"Aye, my Lady, I fear it is."

"I feared as much," Jocelyn sighed, lifting the hem of her fine gown to make her way back down to the yard.

It was time, to once again, greet a party of strangers, when she had only just sent the previous group on their way.

"I am taking you with me, Tomas," Jocelyn ordered, glancing at him over her shoulder once she reached the stairs.

She was too annoyed to do this alone.

"I?" Tomas muttered, not wanting to so closely take part of such attention.

"Aye, you will be by my side in this, make conversation and take a bit of the obligation from me. I cannot force myself to smile and be hospitable for a minute longer."

He'd kept close to her in the past, but never in the way she was implying. Tomas was the captain of her guard, he was to be there to watch over the woman and make certain she was safe with her company, not become a part of the entertainment.

"If I must be subject to this, then so will you be. I am tired of being the center of attention, perhaps you might add a bit to the conversation or even take this next tormenter about the grounds yourself so I might be left to my own for a time." She reached out and took his arm when Tomas joined her, determined to keep him within reach.

"As you wish it," Tomas obliged, hardly looking forward to the task, but if it would make her happy, he would see it done.

Jocelyn and Tomas reached the yard as the call of welcome thundered through the air. Her eyes unwillingly turned to the gate as another memory threatened to overrun her.

Again she was stepping back into the tender hold of years past.

* * * *

After the fighting subsided and the wounded were being cared for, Jocelyn's family gathered in her parents' chamber. They gathered together, desperately clinging to the hope that the youngest of their family would win the battle she waged with the illness that ravaged her body.

Poor Zoe was weak from the siege. Weary of fighting, but struggling to live for those she loved who were huddled about her.

In spite of the pleas from her family and all the best efforts of the healer, dear Zoe had not the strength within her to last the night.

Jocelyn vividly remembered the rain of the day that followed. The relentless onslaught of moisture splattered upon them all as her family led the party of mourners from the small cemetery and back to the shelter of the keep.

So many had died due to the selfish greed of another.

She recalled the thunder as it seemed to lament the passing of one so young. It was the very echoing of her own broken heart, the rain her own unyielding tears, and no matter the effort, she could not contain them.

Jocelyn stood in the hall for as long as she could manage. She was struggling to be strong for her mother and sister, but the dam she'd built about her heart was threatening to burst, putting her in motion.

Silent tears she would give freely, it was the threat of what was coming that turned her from her kin.

Jocelyn followed her feet to the door.

Not caring that the heavens were weeping, she fled for the yard, stopping midway down the outer stairs when she caught sight of her cousin Meredith.

Meredith was standing in the rain, her eyes fixed on the gate as though at any moment the man who left her would return.

Jocelyn learned that very morning that Cody returned to his kin, leaving Meredith behind, for it was at her own request that he left. It seemed his mother was in dire need of her son and Meredith refused to stand in the way. In knowing that without the love of her son, Cody's mother would suffer greatly, Meredith sent the man she cherished away.

Jocelyn finished her descent, closing the distance between herself and Meredith, wrapped her arms about her cousin and rested her chin on her shoulder. Nothing needed to be said between them, Jocelyn only knew that as she hurt, so did Meredith.

They stood in the rain clinging to one another. Their eyes looking to the blurred horizon, waiting for all they had lost to somehow manage to find its way back.

* * * *

Jocelyn pulled herself from the horrid memory before the tears began flowing and looked to the party of men approaching her home.

It was told to her by their herald that the group hailed from Summerly and apparently came under the same guise as all the others. They were here seeking shelter and hospitality.

In her mind, Jocelyn knew better than to believe this was all they were after.

She would very shortly be certain of it for the group was near the gate and would soon fill her yard.

Mortan approached the towering keep, the thundering call of welcome easing away a bit of the ache to his travel-worn body.

Self-consciously he ran a hand through his graying windblown hair and smoothed his beard of the same color. He pulled back his shoulders and made himself look as though he felt years younger than he was in truth.

He was ailing and longed for a much needed rest after such a tedious trek.

Mortan needed this alliance; he needed it more than he cared to admit.

He'd written to Robin, Lord Milberk, asking for the hand of his daughter only to be answered that the girl had a mind of her own, such a decision would be made by her.

The news left Mortan where he sat now, stiff and aching as he looked down at the auburn haired angel before him.

Mortan feared she would see through his facade and know him for the man he was. In truth, he was old, feeble and well past the use of a woman such as she.

His wife had passed years ago, leaving him alone to raise their six children, their son Tristan and five daughters who would soon be in need of husbands, husbands he would never be able to supply for them. If he had not the sum to provide a gift to prospective suitors, the care of his daughters would forever be entrusted to him. That, as well, was a burden he could no longer carry.

"My Lord Summerly, it is a pleasure to make your acquaintance," Jocelyn called out, cheerfully offering her best greeting to the aged lord sitting atop his mount.

The lady was speaking to him, her sweet voice pulling Mortan from his rambling thoughts.

Her hand extended in greeting, forcing Mortan to acknowledge that he'd heard her.

"As the pleasure is all mine, Lady Artois." He dismounted, forcing his limbs to hold his weight, trying for all he was worth to look as though it was not a struggle for them to do so.

"We are traveling home, Lady, and I would pray that it would not be an imposition for us to shelter within your walls to rest?" Mortan asked, not wanting to give her any inclination of his true intentions for seeking shelter in her magnificent home.

Mortan took her hand and held it for a fleeting moment in his own. He needed her acceptance just as he needed air to breathe.

"Not at all, my Lord, you are welcome here." Jocelyn gave the old man a kind smile, taking relief in the certainty that he couldn't be as the others.

Mortan smiled when she gave him a slight bow, gesturing with a silken clad arm to the stairs that would lead them to the keep. She then turned and led the way, followed closely by a stout pale haired man, who from his dress, Mortan could clearly see was the captain of Artois.

Had she a need to keep her captain so close?

"Have you traveled far?" Jocelyn asked when they reached the great room of the castle.

Mortan was propelled toward a cluster of chairs near the hearth. The sight of rest filling him with blessed relief. He knew not how long his shaking legs would offer support.

"Aye, I winter near the border. I have family there," he lied, he and his men had come directly from Summerly. The only family he had left were those he'd left at his dwindling keep.

"Truly? It has been ages since I have been so far from home." Jocelyn motioned for him to sit, eyeing him carefully when he sat himself down in the high back chair and forced himself not to rub his aching limbs.

She could clearly see he was exhausted and in need of a comfortable rest.

"Aye, but now it is time for me to journey home where the remainder of my family is waiting. The journey has taken longer than I anticipated as the weather has not been kind until only just recently." Mortan rested his hands on his lap and stretched out his fingers, even they ached from holding the reins of his mount.

Perhaps it should have been his son who came on this errand. Alas, Tristan didn't know the sad state in which his inheritance rested. Mortan wanted so badly to do the task himself, he was not accustomed to being looked after as though he were a decrepit old man.

Mortan alone created this mess of problems and it was only just that he alone found a way out of them.

"Perhaps I will leave you to your rest; surely you must be fatigued from your travels. Tomas will send the steward to you, if there is anything you need, do not hesitate to ask," Jocelyn graciously supplied.

She was more than ready for a bit of fresh air to call her very own and from the look of Tomas standing back with his arms folded and offering nothing to the silence about them, this was just as good a time as any to seek her solitude and allow her new guest to rest.

Mortan watched her grant him a warm smile and a bow before excusing herself, but not before she gave an unmistakable glare to the man he presumed was Tomas and then she was gone.

"Come with me Lord Summerly, I will take you to your Chamber myself as it seems I have upset my mistress and will be wise to avoid her for the time being." Tomas gave the man help in standing and slowly led him to the stairs.

Mortan allowed the captain to take him to the upper level of the keep and down a long corridor to a spacious room where his own pages were already busy arranging their master's belongings.

"My thanks," Mortan offered, then watched the man go, his brow furrowed slightly as he pondered over the look she'd given her captain and the comment Tomas then made about his mistress.

There was a kind of unspoken intimacy between them.

Was there a reason why the Lady of Artois was still unmarried? Did the captain have something to do with it?

Jocelyn waited just outside the door to the great hall; her arms folded, her eyes fixed on a mass of men seeing to horses and baggage in the dust-ridden yard below.

It was a party that would surely accompany a traveling lord such as her guest. Now they were in her care, to feed and shelter just as she had so many others.

Tomas appeared only a handful of moments later, took one look at her and whistled between his teeth.

He attempted to return to the great room, but Jocelyn quickly caught hold of his arm, taking him captive.

“I thank you for your assistance, I brought you with me for your help not so you could look on like a twit,” she accused, scowling at Tomas in annoyance.

“I thought of nothing to say to the man. You had things well in hand.” Tomas came to stand beside her when she released the hold she had on him, studying her face with concern.

She was drawn and irritated, more so than he’d seen in a very long time.

“He is not like the others is he?” Jocelyn asked in near desperation.

She felt the man wasn’t as all the others; she only longed to be certain before she fully put her guard down.

“I dare say he is not. He seems to be traveling as he said. Are you well, Jo?” Tomas inquired, noticing that the pallor of her skin was slightly paler than usual.

He knew the last few months had been hard on her. Tomas could hardly blame her for being leery of these men who enthusiastically arrived at Artois.

They came slowly at first, these *suitors* who sought her hand. There were two in the fall and a handful throughout the winter, but it seemed as soon as the spring and summer months were upon them, Artois was swarmed with a throng of men who were all after one thing.

Most of them were hardly shy about admitting their true intentions and were reluctant to leave even when Jocelyn wholeheartedly dismissed them.

"Aye, I am well…I would only have one day, Tomas. One day all to myself." She turned and gave him a small smile before rolling her eyes heavenward when he stood shaking his pale head at her.

It was as though he was telling her she would have it in time, but certainly not this day.

"He will not stay long," Jocelyn stated, as if doing so would make it true.

"Perhaps not," Tomas assured, though he feared the man was in need of a good rest.

Lord Summerly was tired from his travels. Tomas knew he would be here longer than Jocelyn wanted, but he chose to keep that thought to himself.

A fortnight later Jocelyn stood outside Lord Summerly's chamber, listening to the low voice of the healer as he conversed with the aged man.

Five days ago he'd fallen ill and was unable to leave the confines of his bed.

She'd pleaded with the man to let the healer come to him, but the old fool was stubborn to a fault refusing, until only moments ago.

She'd learned a great deal about Mortan since he arrived. His wife had passed years ago and his spinster sister was now helping him raise his son and five daughters.

Lord Summerly also told her a great deal about his home. It seemed to be a great holding, beautiful and vast, its grounds spacious, its walls well-fortified.

Jocelyn could tell by the way he spoke of it that he was terribly fond of his home.

She nodded to the healer when he emerged, wanting nothing but the best of news from the man.

"I expect he will be well in a matter of days, it seems his travels have worn on him more than he might have anticipated," the healer supplied, tipping his head at her before making his way down the corridor.

Jocelyn watched him go before tapping lightly on Lord Summerly's door; she then let herself in without waiting for his reply.

"I am told you will be well in no time," she announced, offering the man a bright smile.

He looked years older to her at that moment. Propped up on a mound of pillows, his hair tousled, his face pale and drawn. Even his eyes were dimmed by his ailment.

"Will you not let me send for your son?" Jocelyn asked as she'd done so many times before.

"Nay, I would not trouble him, my dear." Mortan shook his head then turned from her, looking slightly ashamed of the trouble he was causing.

"Your sister then, surely you would feel more yourself if a member of your family was with you," she suggested, crossing the room to stand beside his bed.

Jocelyn knew if she was ill, she would want nothing more than to have her family by her side.

"Nay, I will be well far before they could arrive. You are kind to offer, but I fear I have burdened you enough as it is. You must know I am sorry for the trouble I am causing."

"Aw, my Lord, you were a burden when you first arrived, but I must say I have grown rather fond of you," Jocelyn teased, hoping to help him feel at ease. "No more apologies, I fear you are considered a friend now and I was raised to care for my friends."

"My Lady," Tomas called from the doorway, gaining her attention at once. "Forgive me, but there are riders approaching."

Jocelyn felt herself sigh against her will and tried to mask her annoyance when she offered a warm smile to Lord Summerly.

"Rest, I have it on good authority that you will be better in no time at all. My healer has never been wrong." With that said, she left the room to follow Tomas to the yard.

"Know you who it is?" Jocelyn asked, longing for him to tell her it was her kin approaching, even as she knew they were not due to arrive until the end of the month.

"Nay." Tomas glanced at her when they left the hall and he came to walk beside her.

"I would think no less of you if you chose to close the gate," he assured her.

"I would think less of me," Jocelyn answered, even as she contemplated the idea.

She owed these travelers nothing, not her hospitality or her hand in marriage for that matter.

"The order is yours to give, Jo," Tomas reminded, wishing it was his order to give. He would send the group packing with very little hesitation.

Artois was already granting shelter to Summerly, they needed no further company to hinder them.

They descended the stairs to the sound of a number of hooves thundering toward them.

"I wish to go for a hunt in the morning," Jocelyn whispered, sounding as though she was speaking to herself and not to the man walking beside her.

"Jo?" Tomas asked, not sure he heard her correctly.

It was an odd comment to make when one was rushing to greet further guests.

"Take me for a hunt in the morning. It has been months since I have ridden out alone, without anyone to hinder me, or conversation to obligate me. I just need to be alone."

She felt the walls of her home closing in around her. Jocelyn had been confined to the keep since Lord Summerly arrived and now with whoever was arriving at her gate, she knew she would never last unless she had a bit of time to herself.

"Aye, you know I would take you whenever you would ask it of me." Tomas looked at her in concern, hoping her family would make haste.

She seemed to be clinging to a very thin rope, drawn and weary and desperately seeking a bit of her life that was forced to be left behind when she became the Lady of Artois.

Her father had been reluctant to let her go, but even so, Robin could never have known this would be how her life would be lived. Jocelyn passed her days more like an innkeeper than the mistress of a holding such as Artois.

"Are you well, Jo?" Tomas asked, hearing the announcing call from without the gate as the party asked for permission to enter, permission that could not be given without the consent of the woman standing beside him.

Alas, at that moment, Tomas was more concerned for her well-being than the fact that someone was waiting outside the gate.

"I know not. If it is yet another come to bid for my hand, I will surely run him through," Jocelyn vowed, never looking at him as she spoke.

She was more than capable of completing such a task and Tomas knew as much.

"What would you have me do?"

"Just stay with me and open your mouth this time, even if you have nothing to say," Jocelyn softly ordered, nodding to the herald, who instantly gave the call of welcome, allowing the gates to open.

The barrier squealed on its hinges when the gate was pulled back, permitting the waiting group to approach.

"Aye…and take you hunting in the morning," Tomas reminded, giving her a half smile when she turned to look at him.

Jocelyn returned his smile before turning to face whoever was now coming to call on her.

With the promise of a bit of time of her own upon the morrow, Jocelyn felt certain she could meet this challenge head on, and defeat it as quickly as was possible.

No amount of planning could have prepared her for the man who rode through her gate.

He was a tower of a man, dark and confident. His piercing brown eyes seemed to bore through her, causing her skin to break out in goose bumps and her knees to weaken.

It was a feeling she hadn't felt for years, a feeling that died along with the dear man who caused it.

Every thought of solitude fled from her mind as the man drew rein before her and dismounted.

Jocelyn's head hardly reached his shoulder as he stood before her, pulling his gloves from his hands, then boldly reaching out to take her hand in his.

"Sir Rhyes, at your service, my Lady." He kissed her hand, then offered her a low bow, his deep brown eyes never giving up the hold he possessed on hers.

"Jocelyn of Artois, welcome." She knew she was speaking, but it seemed she'd lost the ability to hear her own voice and prayed she wasn't sounding like a fool.

"My thanks, Lady. I would never impose, but rumors of you have traveled far and I could not help but come to Artois and see for myself if they were true!" Rhyes exclaimed, still holding her hand captive.

"Rumors?" Jocelyn questioned, more than happy to hold his hand for as long as he saw fit to do so.

"Aye, wild rumors of a foul, shrieking shrew of a woman who would sooner rip a man's head from his shoulders than lose hold of her freedom. Thousands of men she has turned from her gates, rich and poor alike and each and every one scarred for life from her horridness."

"I beg your pardon?" Jocelyn snapped, coming back to herself at once.

She yanked her hand from his, the strange spell he'd woven over her broken as though it had never been.

"How dare you!" Jocelyn blurted, grateful to have possession of her wits once more.

Tomas was nearly between them, his anger with the man's insulting words vivid on his face.

"I speak only in jest," Rhyes laughed, placing his hand on the shoulder of her loyal captain as though they were the best of mates.

The rich merry tones of his voice caused Jocelyn's knees to weaken against their will. How was it possible for him to vex her and then turn her again to mush so swiftly?

"I see no humor in such an insult," Tomas threw at him, keeping his hand boldly resting on the hilt of his sword as he shook Rhyes hand off his shoulder only to have it return again, irritating Tomas all the more.

"No insult, friend. If you must know I have, in truth, heard a great deal of rumors and not a one of them did your lady justice. To be honest, I doubted such a lady could exist, but it seems I was mistaken, for here you stand." Rhyes gave her another bow, then stood before her, seeming to wait for her reply.

Jocelyn watched Tomas push Rhyes hand aside and relax slightly with his words, but her temper was sparked. She would not be made a fool of, not at the expense of any man.

"Many a man has entered these gates, Sir, and many a man I have sent packing. If you count yourself to be the same as these lackwits who have entered my walls, seeking their fortune through a meek and unsuspecting woman, then you are greatly mistaken.

"I would bid you good day before it is you who is insulted. You may pass the night in the barracks with your men and upon the morrow you will leave my walls." She turned on her heel and left him where he stood.

Her heart pounding in her chest, her breath stolen from her lungs, causing her to fear that she would never breathe again.

Tomas folded his arms and looked to the man waiting to see his insult with Jocelyn's harsh words, but Rhyes never flinched.

If anything, his smile only grew in size.

Chapter Two

Well before the sun was preparing to rise, Jocelyn descended the outer stairs of the keep.

Her long auburn hair was braided and tucked up beneath a man's cap, her usual feminine attire replaced with thick woolen hose and a plain tunic. Her boots rose nearly to her knees and the thick belt at her waist sported her hunting knife and sword.

The thick dark cloak draped about her narrow shoulders blocked the chill of early morning as she quickly made her way to the stables to meet Tomas.

"Good morrow, Jo," Tomas greeted when he caught sight of her approaching. His pale blonde hair lit by the glow of the torches.

Tomas took hold of her horse by his reins and led the beast to the lady.

"Good morrow. I have a feeling it will be a grand morning indeed." Jocelyn reached out and patted the animal upon the neck, feeling a wide smile creep over her mouth with the prospect of a morning of solitude.

Her father would be terribly angry with her if he even had the smallest inclination that she was going on a hunt without the master huntsman and a proper escort.

In his mind, as she was a lady and his daughter, Jocelyn should not even think of hunting without the appropriate protection of experienced men.

Alas, her father wasn't here and Tomas was all the protection she needed.

"You look more yourself," Tomas mused when she reached out to take her quiver and bow from a yawning page.

Jocelyn shrugged the quiver effortlessly over her shoulder and smiled brightly at Tomas.

"Aye, I fear all I need is a bit of fresh air."

Tomas nodded his agreement and helped her into her saddle before mounting his own horse.

Within moments, they left the confines of the yard and surrounding village to enter the woods beyond.

Their ears honed in on their surroundings, as the first dim gray light of morning crept in around them.

Jocelyn looked to the shadows of trees and boulders as their horses meandered forward. She'd hunted many a time with her father, then they used dogs to force their prey from hiding. She'd never been fond of hunting in such a fashion, she took pleasure in finding her prey on her own, not startling it from seclusion with a pack of yipping dogs.

"There," Tomas whispered, pointing with his bow to a clearing just ahead of where they rode.

A mighty stag was feasting on the dew-drenched grass of the clearing.

For a moment, it seemed he sensed their eyes on him for he lifted his head, ears twitching and turning to hear the slightest sound. When the stag was satisfied that he was alone, he went back to grazing on his fine morning meal.

In perfect unison she and Tomas pulled an arrow from their quivers, placed it against the string of their bow and pulled back, aiming at the unsuspecting animal.

Jocelyn listened for Tomas to release his breath, telling her he was ready to let his arrow fly.

"Good morrow," a man's voice came from behind them.

The loud greeting startled the stag, causing his head to shoot up, his eyes fixed on them for but a second before he bolted.

Both Jocelyn and Tomas let their arrows fly. Tomas managed to hit his mark, striking the animal in the neck falling the beast, while Jocelyn's arrow missed horribly, striking a tree in the distance.

"Good shot!" the man complimented, his voice suddenly all too familiar. "Had I seen the animal, I would not have said anything."

Jocelyn turned on him, looking back over her shoulder at the lout, her green eyes flashing sparks.

"I thought I asked you to leave!" she fumed, pulling another arrow from her quiver and placed it in her bow. She lifted the weapon, aiming it deliberately at the intruder.

She would never shoot the man, but that didn't stop the thought from crossing her mind.

"Am I mistaken?" she asked when he said nothing in answer to her question.

Rhyes stared at her in blunt shock. He'd thought it was a man hunting alongside the captain of Artois's guard, not the lady herself.

"Jocelyn?" Rhyes questioned in shock, squinting at her to make certain his eyes weren't playing tricks on him.

"Lady Artois, friend," Tomas barked, turning his mount to place the beast between the unwanted guest and his lady.

"Aye…Lady, you are dressed as a man," Rhyes stated, as though he might truly think she didn't know how she was dressed.

"As are you," Jocelyn remarked, turning her horse to face him, tipping her chin up to get a better look at his stunned countenance from beneath her cap.

"Aye, but you are a woman," Rhyes stated, certain he didn't need to inform her as much, yet it seemed odd to him that she would be dressed in such a way.

"And it would seem that you are the most observant of men," Jocelyn mocked just as her master huntsman and a small group of riders appeared through the trees.

"Good morrow my Lady," the huntsman greeted, looking slightly guilty when their eyes met.

"Was it you who brought this man into my forest?" Jocelyn asked, resting her bow on her lap as to not look quite so threatening.

"Aye, I saw no harm in an early morning hunt, I knew not you would be out this day." He bowed his head at her, realizing his great mistake. He should have cleared the hunting party with her before taking the stranger out.

Jocelyn gave the apologetic huntsman a nod and glanced over her shoulder to where the stag lay in the long grass.

"Take care of the stag, Tomas and I will see Sir Rhyes back to the keep." What was done was done; neither of them would gain anything if she reprimanded him.

It was obvious to her that the huntsman knew he was in the wrong, she would leave it as it was for the time being.

"Come, Sir, it is time you were on your way." Jocelyn spurred her mount forward, giving Rhyes no choice but to turn his horse and fall in beside her.

"I am not wholly in the wrong," Rhyes stated after a moment of silence.

"For what, Sir? Are you not in the wrong for not leaving when asked? Or are you not wrong for hunting in my forest without my permission?" she glared at him briefly before passing her bow and arrow to Tomas when he took his place on the other side of her mount.

"I was under the impression the huntsmen cleared the hunt with his lady. If I remember correctly, you gave me until the morrow. If I am not mistaken, the sun has not yet crested over the horizon."

"It will before we are able to pass through the gates and then Sir, you will be in the wrong," Jocelyn snapped.

She was irritated with the slight fluttering of her heart that persisted in remaining even after her nerves had calmed.

Was it because he was handsome? Or that he was younger than any of the others who came calling on her?

What did it matter, he was as all the others, he'd bluntly confessed to being such a man and she would see him gone.

"Are you always this disagreeable? Is she always this disagreeable?" Rhyes asked to Tomas when she gave him no answer.

Tomas only grunted and gave him a glare of his own.

There was something about this man that bit at Tomas' nerves. Rhyes was too handsome and witty, but there was something more, something he'd seen the day before when the man arrived at Artois.

Perhaps it was the hotheaded arrogance of a man who is accustomed to acquiring that which he seeks that aggravated Tomas?

"I am only disagreeable when provoked," Jocelyn responded when it seemed Tomas was near ready to snap. "You are enough to irritate even the most timid of women."

"Then you should have little dispute with me for I dare say you are far from a timid woman. I have never known a woman who deliberately dresses as a man. Do you do so often, for I must say I am intrigued?"

Jocelyn bit her bottom lip and controlled the urge to suck in a mighty breath and take her bow back from Tomas.

"Perhaps you should pull yourself away from court a bit more often than you do. That is where you hail from is it not?" Jocelyn asked.

She felt he would fit well in court. She could see Rhyes there, complimenting, teasing and making a full spectacle of himself.

"I have spent my time in court, Lady. I will not deny it. I have also traveled abroad; I have seen many a great thing and many a remarkable woman. Still, I am safe in saying I have never seen a woman such as yourself." Rhyes tipped his head at her, his gaze never leaving her face as the wall came into view.

Jocelyn rolled her eyes and bit down harder on her lip, attempting to control her mouth from saying something highly insulting. All the while, she was trying to discern if he was in truth curious about her, or mocking her.

She'd always dressed as a man when she hunted; it seemed right in her mind. Why ruin a perfectly good gown when it mattered not what became of the hose and tunic she wore.

"I think you have said enough," Tomas informed him, just as the sun crept up over the skyline, blinding them momentarily with its golden light.

"I hardly meant to offend," Rhyes assured them both, but it seemed the damage was already done.

"You have offered offence from the very moment you arrived. Had I no self-control I would have run you through the very moment you uttered a word!" Tomas yelled, his temper turning his face crimson.

"The only offence I have offered was in jest, I would never insult a lady in truth, namely a lady as lovely as Lady Artois," Rhyes defended, his own temper beginning to flair.

"Jest or no, I believe there to be truth in your words, otherwise, they would never have been spoken!" Tomas accused.

"It is now you who offers insult, man!" Rhyes blurted, his temper snapping. "If you were more than a lowly servant, I would challenge you for such a remark."

"Then offer your challenge, Sir, for I am more than able to accept!" Tomas yelled back.

He'd won his spurs as a youth, Tomas was more than a fit opponent for this pompous knight.

"Enough!" Jocelyn broke in before the challenge could be issued.

The last thing she needed now was the two of them fighting to uphold their tarnished honor.

"Truly the two of you, you sound as children not grown men," she scolded, casting Tomas a glare.

"If I have truly offered insult, Lady, allow me to redeem myself," Rhyes pleaded.

His statement caused Jocelyn to turn and look at him, his eyes instantly captivating her with his heartfelt plea.

"I never meant to insult, it is a terrible flaw of mine to use humor to mask my nerves.

"I would like nothing more than to remain awhile and mend my tarnished name. I could not leave knowing you think ill of me," Rhyes pleaded, hoping she would accept so he might fix what he'd done.

Jocelyn turned her eyes back to the gate as they approached, questioning fully what her racing mind was thinking. She wasn't brought up to be cruel and unforgiving. It was so far from her nature not to give a being a second chance.

She took a deep breath as they passed into the yard, shook her head for she knew she was a fool and rolled her eyes just for good measure.

"Very well," she sighed.

"Jo…truly you cannot let him stay," Tomas protested, his stomach tying into a thick knot.

"But as your punishment, and until I trust you, you will pass your nights in the barracks with your men. You must give me your word that while you reside within my walls, you will refrain from associating me with marriage. Is this understood?" she asked, scowling at Rhyes when he dismounted, and crossed to where she sat on her mount.

Rhyes boldly took hold of her about the waist and helped her to her feet, leaving his hands to linger on her waist for a bit longer than was necessary.

"Understood," Rhyes whispered, giving an intimacy to their exchange that truly didn't exist.

"Good," Jocelyn muttered, taking a step back when her horse was led away.

"Good," Rhyes mimicked, his penetrating eyes still fixed on hers, causing her to all but lose herself in his gaze.

"Now go away," Jocelyn ordered, after a moment of struggling to find her voice.

She couldn't focus when he was looking at her in such a way.

Rhyes gave her a bow and left, following his feet to the barracks to no doubt tell his men that they would not be leaving after all.

Rhyes changed his clothes within the open sleeping quarters of the barracks, then made his way to the hall to break his fast.

Much to his surprise, Jocelyn never appeared for the morning meal. Instead, a tray of food was retrieved by her maidservant and ushered upstairs.

He rested his elbows on the table and smiled at Tomas who was obviously glaring at him from where he sat with the other men of his rank.

The captain clearly didn't like him.

Rhyes could hardly blame him. Tomas seemed terribly loyal to his mistress even to the point of calling her by a dear nickname.

Such a thing was far from unheard of, but more unlikely when it was a man and a woman.

Rhyes shoved the thought to the back of his mind and downed the contents of his goblet before leaving the table to make his way from the room.

He would see to his men, then perhaps have a look around the grounds.

From what he'd seen thus far, the keep was agreeable to his tastes, vast and well kept. He could see himself here. He could see himself happy and content. Not only that, Rhyes could see himself wed to a woman such as Jocelyn. She possessed fire as well as a forgiving heart.

She was a good woman, what more could a man ask for?

It was near three hours later when Rhyes entered the seclusion of the gardens, taking in the vast abundance of herbs in the space near the kitchen and the array of blooming flowers and leaf-ridden trees that sprouted up the farther he meandered away from the keep.

Like everything else at Artois, the garden was well cared for, hardly a surprise to him after his morning of roaming the grounds.

The lady had an eye for detail, it seemed there was nothing that was overlooked.

"Tomas tells me you have been wandering the grounds," Jocelyn's voice came from the distance where she was standing by a pond.

Jocelyn's arms were folded across the front of her flowing violet gown, her hair pulled back from her face by a crowning braid that was adorned with a string of beads strung on a silver chain.

There was no doubt in his mind that he would never grow weary of such a sight as the lovely woman who stood in the distance.

"Aye, your good captain has kept his eye on me has he?" Rhyes inquired with a light smile.

“Tell me Sir, do you approve of my work? I am a mere woman after all.” Jocelyn tipped her head at him then folded her arms a bit tighter when he approached.

“Aye, I was only just thinking to myself of what a magnificent job you have done,” he praised, crossing the distance to where she stood.

“I like you better dressed as a woman,” Rhyes commented, his mouth twitching into a wide smile with the sight of the crimson hue that took over her cheeks.

“You are not allowed to like me at all. Or have you forgotten?” She turned to the pond, watching absently as a fish leapt from the water to consume an unfortunate insect.

“So I have been told.” Rhyes came to stand beside her, gazing as she did at the mirror-like surface of the water before them.

“I could not help but notice that you have men from Summerly roaming around within your walls,” Rhyes remarked.

“You *are* observant,” Jocelyn taunted, dropping her hands to her sides as she turned and began walking back the way he’d only just come.

In her retreat, she gave him no choice but to follow her.

"Their master fell ill only days after he arrived," Jocelyn explained, deciding there was little use in being coy with him.

She had nothing to hide.

"Tristan is here?" Rhyes asked in slight shock.

He was hoping to have no competition in his task, namely that of a man he knew.

"Nay, his father. I pleaded with him to allow me to send for his son, but he refused the offer. Perhaps I should have ignored his wishes and sent for him anyway," she mused, tipping her head up at the midday sun, allowing its rays to kiss her upturned face as they slowly walked.

"Nay, the Summerly's are tough, proud people. I have no doubt he will be up and well in no time."

"You seem to know his son, but do you know Lord Summerly as well?" Jocelyn asked, stopping to face him.

"Nay, though I do know his son…knew his son would be more true. It has been years since I have been in Tristan's company.

"We fostered together as lads. The last I knew of Tristan, he'd won his spurs and was preparing to return home to Summerly. This was years ago only just after Lady Summerly became ill." Rhyes gave her a warm smile and allowed himself to imagine them passing their days in like fashion for years and years to come.

Such a thing was easy enough to imagine, he only hoped then that talk would not be of another man.

"I have known Lord Summerly for only a short time, but he seems a good man, kind and honorable, a great deal like my own father," Jocelyn replied, a kind of homesick lump clogging her heart.

Jocelyn seemed miles away at that moment, a soft smile creeping over her mouth as fond memories fluttered through her mind.

"I have never met Robin of Milberk, tell me—" he was cut short by the pale haired Tomas who was running down the pathway, a rolled bit of parchment in his hand.

"Jo, I have news from your family!" Tomas announced, passing the missive to her, but not before scowling at Rhyes to let him know he was displeased to find them together.

"How far are they from Artois?" she asked, giving Rhyes a quick bow to excuse herself before she left with Tomas.

"The messenger informed me they are not a whole week's journey," Tomas answered before dropping his voice to a whisper, a whisper that Rhyes clearly heard. "What do you alone with that man?"

"He was walking the garden, Tomas, as I was," Jocelyn whispered back. "What would you have me do, run from him?"

"I do not trust him, Jo."

"Nor do I, this is why I was making my way back to the yard. If we have only a week there is much left we have to do—"

Rhyes could hear nothing after that and remained where she left him, contemplating the two of them as they faded from sight.

Were they more than mere Lady and captain?

He sensed they were friends, but was it more than that?

Perhaps it was time he look a little deeper into their strange relationship and see what it was he could discover before her kin arrived.

Chapter Three

Mortan sat beside Jocelyn in the great hall of Artois, listening with disdain as the handsome Rhyes told fascinating stories of his many exploits.

The later the hour grew, the more Mortan began to wonder how he was ever going to compete with this man. Rhyes was young and striking, in the prime of his life, not knocking loudly on deaths door.

"I would have won the melee that day, but you see a comrade of mine was desperately seeking the good favor of his lady, and so, as I had nothing to gain from winning, I allowed him to best me. They are now happily wed with a brood of children," Rhyes concluded, a bright smile fixed to his face.

"Truly?" Jocelyn questioned.

She was clearly skeptical that this man would do any such thing as taking second place to anyone.

"Aye, do you not believe my tale?" Rhyes asked, his smile never wavering.

"I think it is just that," Tomas broke in, "a tale."

"It is true as I stand before you now. I honor my friendships, captain, as it seems you do as well. Tell me…how long have you been in service to the lovely Lady Artois?" Rhyes inquired, his voice was smooth even as he picked at something that was none of his concern.

Mortan could sense Rhyes was digging at the relationship between the captain and his mistress. Perhaps it was the same inkling Mortan was having concerning the lady and the man she kept close by her.

They were close, but surely there was nothing more between them than friendship.

"I served her father before I served his daughter. I practically watched her grow up, Sir. What business is it of yours who her friends are, or my own?" Tomas ranted, looking as though he was ready to rush to his feet at any moment.

"Saints preserve us all," Jocelyn muttered and reached out to place her hand over Mortan's when the two men commenced in bellowing at one another.

Tomas was suddenly standing before Rhyes, each of them shouting to be heard above the ranting of the other.

"I can bear no more of this," she confessed to Mortan.

The two men had only just finished arguing before Rhyes began his heroic tale. It would be a tedious night if this was how they chose to behave.

"Would you be so kind as to escort me to my chamber, my Lord? I would rather seek my rest than listen to a moment longer of their bickering."

"It would be my pleasure." Mortan slowly gained his feet and offered her his arm, leaving the two men to their quarreling.

He had a mind to think it would be a good while before either of them were missed, for the shouting that was now taking place was deafening even to his ears.

"You seem to be feeling much more like yourself," Jocelyn observed while they slowly climbed the stairs.

"I fear I will never be as I once was my dear, but for the man I am now, I must say I cannot complain," he remarked, grateful she wasn't looking at him for she would have seen his face drawn in deep concentration.

"I have the feeling I have worn out my welcome," Mortan stated once they reached the corridor.

"Nay, my Lord. I would like nothing more than for you to meet my father. My family will arrive any day now, I know he would be happy to make your acquaintance," Jocelyn assured him.

Alas, the ruckus coming from the hall below them told Mortan he would have to come up with a new means to free himself of his rival.

He was no match for Sir Rhyes and he had the feeling that if the man was given enough time, the charming lady beside him would fall sway to Rhyes' charms and all would be lost.

"I long for my kin as you do, it is time I returned home. Perhaps one day you might come to Summerly. I would love nothing more than to see you within the walls of my home," Mortan suggested, certain he would never see such a woman at Summerly.

They came to a stop before her door just as a loud crash echoed up the stairwell.

Jocelyn sighed at the sound of something breaking below. The shouting didn't cease and she could only shake her head before reaching up to kiss Mortan on the cheek and bid him goodnight.

"Pleasant sleep," she offered, shaking her head again when another loud crash added to the ruckus in the great hall.

"Perhaps I might return to the hall and make certain they both still live," Mortan suggested, slightly hoping Tomas would free them all of Sir Rhyes.

That would be a great blessing indeed.

"Nay, let them squabble. I would rather they get it done and over with, I am tired of their bickering." Jocelyn gave him a small smile and disappeared within her chamber.

Mortan respected her wishes and made his way to his own chamber, sending his squire to the barracks to inform his men that they would leave at first light.

He needed to return to Summerly with all haste. He needed to find a way to secure his future as well as the future of his son and daughters.

It was obvious to Mortan that he could no longer do so here.

Mortan longed to remove Jocelyn from the walls of Artois; he needed her to see how badly she was needed at Summerly.

He not only needed her wealth, but perhaps his daughters could benefit from her kindness. Mortan knew that once Jocelyn saw how she might help them, she would never refuse. It was only a matter of getting Jocelyn to see the situation with her own eyes.

At daybreak, Jocelyn stood in the yard, her arms folded, her head tipped to the side as she looked over the captain of her guard.

Tomas' lip was split in more than one place, he sported a deep cut across the side of his forehead, his right eye was swollen nearly shut and she couldn't help but notice that he'd been limping when he approached her.

"Do not look at me in such a way," Tomas murmured, his words barely audible though his swollen lip.

"In what way am I looking at you?" Jocelyn questioned, wondering slightly if Rhyes looked as abused as Tomas or if her captain had gotten the best of the man.

"I was defending your honor," Tomas informed her, though they both knew better.

It was his own pride he was looking after when it came to Sir Rhyes.

"My honor…hummm. Tell me, my dear friend, is my honor still intact or is it now missing along with your own?" Jocelyn sweetly asked.

She turned from her captain's glare and smiled brightly at Lord Summerly when he approached. He was the only civil company she'd had for the last handful of days and now after seeing Tomas, she was truly sad to see Mortan go.

"I thank you most kindly for your hospitality and kind care for my health." Mortan took hold of her hand and held it tenderly with his own.

"The pleasure is all mine, my Lord. Were my family not arriving, I would beg you take me with you." She glanced at Tomas, a playful smile turning up the corner of her mouth.

"You would never have to beg, my dear, my home is always open to you," Mortan assured her, patting her hand as he spoke.

"Then I will have to come and see it for myself. Safe journey my friend." Jocelyn watched him turn and leave, noting the sorrow in his eyes.

She hadn't noticed such sadness in him until that moment. It had been there last evening, now that she thought of it, Mortan had not been in the most cheerful of moods last night. Certainly he was only lamenting the journey and not returning to his home.

"I will have you know I pounded the twit into the dust," Tomas whispered when Lord Summerly was well out of hearing.

"What else did you pound into the dust in the process? Two of my fine chairs, a leg of my table is broken, not to mention the disarray you caused to the hall because of your petty quarreling. When I asked you to stay with me, this is not what I meant." She watched Lord Summerly's party ride through the gate and forced herself to ignore his mighty sigh.

"Rhyes has done nothing but offend you from the moment he arrived, and yet you have granted him lodgings here. You would tell me his sharp tongue and smooth demeanor impresses you?" Tomas scoffed, clearly shocked with his rebuke for speaking up for her.

"I am willing to grant the man a second chance. I would be obliged if you would kindly do the same. Rhyes has done nothing to offend since he apologized and I refuse to despise him for his past offences."

Jocelyn turned and made her way back to the keep, lifting the hem of her gown as she climbed the stairs.

"You like him!" Tomas blurted in blatant horror, keeping pace with her as she climbed.

"Nay…I am only being a kind hostess," Jocelyn readily assured, even as her mind wondered over his words.

She did like Rhyes. What was there not to like?

She did not as yet trust him as fully as she would like, but he was slowly gaining her attention.

"You would not defend him in such a way if you did not like him," Tomas accused, taking hold of her arm to bring her to a stop midway up the stairs.

Jocelyn scowled at Tomas for a moment then seemed to notice the look of near panic in his pale blue eyes.

"Are you jealous of him, Tomas?" she asked, hardly believing it herself until his face turned a deep crimson.

"Nay…nay! I do not trust him." Tomas released the hold he had on her arm and turned to stomp down the stairs, his limp more apparent now that he was angry.

"I do not trust him," he called again over his shoulder, "and neither should you!"

Jocelyn pursed her lips and silently watched him go.

Tomas had been with her for so long that she knew him better than he cared to believe.

She knew he cared for her; she cared for him as well. Tomas was as dear to her as her own kin; perhaps this was why he felt it was his responsibility to look after her.

When Tomas disappeared from sight, Jocelyn turned and made her way into the hall, her eyes instantly falling on Rhyes where he sat before the hearth. He was taking a moment of ease in one of the two chairs that survived the evening's hostilities.

He was leaning forward, his elbows resting on his knees, his chin cupped in his hands as his dark eyes stared into the vacant hearth.

"Licking your wounds?" Jocelyn inquired, crossing to where Rhyes sat.

He stood slowly, looking for a moment like Lord Summerly, for he moved as though he was aching all over.

Rhyes nodded his head and attempted to smile though his abused face wouldn't allow it. He was as bruised as Tomas, his lips were split, his eyes blackened and a few cuts and scrapes marred his handsome face.

"I dare say Tomas was right, he did pound you into the dust," Jocelyn softly teased, her voice laced with sympathy.

"I underestimated him," Rhyes informed her, gesturing for her to sit in the chair opposite his, which she did for fear he would fall over if he stood much longer.

"For a man of his size and build, he is quick on his feet. Though I must say he walked away with a good deal of abuse." Rhyes again leaned forward in his chair.

The way he chose to sit caused Jocelyn to think his back was ailing him as well.

"The two of you are acting as children," she remarked, studying him a bit closer when he again gazed into the ashes.

"Tomas began the quarrel."

"And you seem to have no problem participating in it. You had every right to walk away," Jocelyn informed him, knowing there was not a man in the whole of the land who could walk away from such a thing.

"I was defending my honor," Rhyes muttered.

"And how is your honor this morning?" she questioned a smile playing across her face when he glanced up at her.

"Sore…and bruised. But, I would do it all again to have you look at me as you do now." He shook his head at her when her smile turned to a scowl and it was her turn to hide her eyes in the ashes of the hearth.

"I fear your captain cares for you," Rhyes offered after a moment of silence.

"Why should he not? I care for him as well…he is as dear to me as my own kin." She shifted in her chair, contemplating the conversation she'd had with Tomas only moments before.

She and Tomas were close, but certainly not in the way Rhyes was implying.

"I fear it is not brotherly affection he holds for you, dearest Jo," Rhyes suggested, his eyes intently fixed on her face.

"Do not call me that," Jocelyn briskly ordered, her stomach quickly tying in knots as her mind rolled his words over and over in her head.

"Tomas calls you Jo," Rhyes defended with a painfully lifted brow.

"I have known him for the whole of my life. He may call me whatever he wishes, Sir. I have known you for but a fortnight and still I am unsure of your intentions.

"You came here a stranger and still you are little more than that to me. Tomas is dear not only to me, but to my family as well. I would ask that you not speak of this matter again." She was more than ready to leave him to his own reflections, but she remained where she sat, her eyes searching the ashes for any distraction she could find.

"Are my intentions truly so masked, Jocelyn. Truly do you not know why I have sought you out?" Rhyes asked.

His voice was so low and smooth it threatened to cause her to tremble.

"You are the same as all the others," Jocelyn mumbled, her girlish thoughts that perhaps this man would be different crumbling into the reality that he was here for one purpose alone.

Why should he not be? Artois is a grand keep.

Why would any man not wish to call it his own?

"You are here for Artois?" she stated, daring to look at him.

Rhyes stood abruptly with the sting of her words and crossed the short distance to where she sat and painfully knelt before her.

"I am not as the other men, Lady. I am here for you," he informed her bluntly.

"When I told you before that I heard rumors of you and that was what brought me here, I spoke truth. I heard tale of a grand and splendid lady who possessed kindness, grace, and beauty. Not only that, but a magnificent keep, one that crazed men to pursue her.

"How many have you turned away?" he asked, but hardly gave her a chance to answer before he reached out and took hold of her hand, forcing her to look at him.

"It is true I have no holdings of my own, but the truth remains…I am here for you, Artois would only be an added blessing to my life if I made an offer that I am not allowed to make within the walls of your home."

"Perhaps I have no desire to wed," Jocelyn lied, her glance wavering slightly as she spoke.

She longed to wed. She longed for the great happiness she'd seen her kinswomen acquire when they wed the man their hearts deemed worthy.

"Do not speak falsely to me. I see what you long for in your eyes. You will marry, you are only waiting for the right man," Rhyes stated, taking her slightly aback with his words.

"What makes you think that you, of all men, is the man I should marry?" Jocelyn asked, pulling on her hands to free them only to find he wouldn't allow it.

"I never said I was. I am simply asking that you give me the opportunity to prove myself.

"Had I been like all the other men, I would have done so already. If I was a horrid being, I would have used all the cunning I possess to petition the king for your hand. As he thinks highly of me, he would have granted my request and then, dearest Jocelyn, you would no longer have a choice. You have been fortunate thus far, that no other has been so favored."

Jocelyn felt her heart drop with his words as every thought she'd ever had for this man abruptly changed.

She was not the sort of woman who could be forced into a marriage that was not of her choosing.

She longed for a life full of love with a man who consumed her heart and soul, not a man who won her through the favor of the king.

"Are you threatening me?" Jocelyn asked, again pulling on her hands, willing them to be free of his hold.

"Nay, I am only telling you that I am not the sort of man who normally takes chances when it comes to that which I desire." His voice was nothing more than a whisper, chilling her skin and adding an edge to the tension in the air surrounding them.

"Jo?" Tomas called from across the great room where he was standing in the doorway, his hand resting on the hilt of his sword.

Jocelyn shook her head and pulled her hands free once she realized Rhyes had eased the hold he had on her.

"Aye," she answered, rising to her feet, suddenly feeling as though she needed a bit of fresh air.

"Your family approaches," Tomas informed her, his eyes slightly hollow when he looked past her to where Rhyes was now standing.

"My thanks," Jocelyn nearly croaked and struggled to compose herself.

Rhyes had hit a nerve with his bold comment and now she was trying to decide whether or not he was the sort of man she could ever fully trust.

Would he take advantage of his position with the king and force her into marriage? Or would he continue on as he was and try to win her on his own?

When Tomas felt as though she was stalling for a moment to conclude the conversation he interrupted, he gave her a slight bow then disappeared through the door.

“I will not be manipulated into marriage, Sir. I will not be treated as a stupid woman who knows nothing of the world around her. I know what a man would gain if he were to wed me, just as I know what I would lose if I were to wed a man who thinks nothing of me beyond the great wealth I would bring him,” Jocelyn informed Rhyes, her back still facing him.

“And I am not the sort of man to take such a woman as yourself for granted,” Rhyes remarked, leaning forward so his words fell evenly into her ear. “I never yield, Lady. Not when the prize is so fine as this.”

Jocelyn turned briskly to face him, her temper pricked with his arrogant words.

Her hand flew on its own, slapping him smartly across his already abused face.

Before he could speak, Jocelyn fled the room, hastily making her way to the yard. Now, more than ever before, she was thankful for her family’s arrival.

Chapter Four

Jocelyn remained in her father's embrace, relishing the security his arms offered and the familiar windblown smell of his skin.

"Are you well, love?" Robin asked after a moment of holding her.

"Aye, I have only missed you terribly," Jocelyn answered, pulling back to smile up at him, hoping he would not see her frazzled nerves. "It has been far too long."

"We would have been here days ago, but I fear your sister had to bring the whole of her chamber," Robin teased when Liza approached, looking as though she'd been pampered the whole of the journey.

The young woman's gown was fresh and clean, her dark hair newly brushed and resting smoothly down the length of her back.

"I'll not look a mess simply because we are traveling," Liza complained before hugging her sister fiercely. "One never knows who they might meet on the road; it is only just that one looks their best."

"One will drive us all mad before our traveling is through," Sarah mused, wondering how her daughter ever became so vain.

Sarah looked her eldest child over before pulling Jocelyn into her arms; grateful they were here at last. Months and months of not seeing her oldest daughter was nearly too much for Sarah to bear.

"You look weary my love," Sarah whispered in her ear before pulling back.

"I have been waiting for you to arrive, that's all." Jocelyn glanced to Tomas as she spoke, clearly noting his pursed lips as she belied her irritation with her present situation.

"I am not the one who is an heiress," Liza ranted to her father, still attempting to defend herself. "I must gain a husband with wealth and one cannot do so looking as a vagabond." She stopped her ranting and stared in the direction of the door and the man who had magically appeared in the doorway of the keep.

"Oh bless me," Liza whispered and self-consciously ran a hand through her hair.

Jocelyn rolled her eyes and took a mighty breath, they were destined to meet Sir Rhyes as it was, they might as well get it over with sooner rather than later.

"Who is this," her mother asked, draping her arm through her daughter's as she spoke, hopeful Jocelyn had put her lost love behind her at last.

Jocelyn beckoned for Rhyes to approach, scowled at her sister and then Tomas before offering the introductions.

"This is Sir Rhyes, recently from the court. He has been with us for the past fortnight." She took another breath when he came to stand beside her, hating the affect he had upon her limbs, causing them to quake and tremble against their will.

"Rhyes this is my family, my father Robin, Lord Milberk, my mother and sister, Liza.

Liza bit her bottom lip and boldly offered him her hand; then struggled to mask a giggle when he kissed her fingers.

"It is a pleasure to meet you, Sir. My sister is blessed indeed to have you in her company." Liza raised her dark brows at him, clearly trying to discern what sort of relationship her sister had with the handsome man.

Robin stepped forward with her words and took hold of Liza's arm, quietly telling her to bite her tongue.

"Your daughter holds you in the highest of regard," Rhyes offered, giving Robin a slight bow. "I am happy to finally make your acquaintance."

"As am I." Robin glanced over his shoulder at Tomas and then back again at Rhyes, his own brow rising in question.

"Has there been trouble?" Robin asked, directing the question at Jocelyn, but it was Tomas who stepped forward with the answer.

"Nay, my Lord, only a difference of opinion. I fear Sir Rhyes and I do not always see eye-to-eye," Tomas supplied, shrugging his shoulders when he spoke as though there was truly nothing more to be said on the matter.

Robin nodded and walked past his daughter to where Rhyes stood and propelled him up the stairs, quietly conversing with the man as they went.

"I have not been to court in years, tell me Sir, what news you have to share," Robin began.

"He seems a fine man," Sarah supplied, her arm still linked through her daughter's.

"Aye, he seems to be." Jocelyn glanced over her shoulder to where Tomas was standing, looking slightly hurt that he'd been so abruptly dismissed by her father.

"What mean you?" Sarah asked, sensing there was something more to the strange feeling swirling around in the air.

Sarah had blamed the tension on the excitement of their arrival, but the masked looks passing between her daughter, Tomas and Sir Rhyes seemed to hold more than a simple glance.

"I have known him for only a short while, there is still much I have to discover concerning who he is. Come, let us go in, surely you are weary. Your chamber has been prepared and I want nothing more than to hear of your travels." Jocelyn took her family in to the hall, saddened when Tomas remained behind in the yard.

She knew he had things to occupy him, but never in the past would he stay behind when her kin came to Artois. Tomas considered himself one of them, a part of the family.

Jocelyn knew she needed to mend what had taken place this last handful of days.

If only she knew where to begin.

Jocelyn patted the neck of her mount from where she stood beside him and struggled to refrain from rolling her eyes as her sister mooned over the visiting knight.

She was beginning to fear the man would never leave, namely now that her family was in residence. Her father had taken a liking to Rhyes and her sister couldn't seem to help but fawn over him from sun up to sun down.

"In truth, I have never seen a finer mount," Liza complimented, her voice soft and sweet. "I dare say he is only lacking when in the company of his master."

"Truly Liza," Jocelyn chastised and shook her head at her sister. "Might we be on our way?" she asked, irritated that it was taking them so long to depart.

If they were going on a hunt, it was well past time they should leave. The master huntsman and his men were already mounted and riding toward the gate.

Liza beamed down at her sister from where she sat in the saddle of her horse before turning the beast to join her father and the rest of the men.

"I apologize for my sister," Jocelyn said as Rhyes approached, leading his horse with him. "She knows not when she has overstepped her bounds."

"There is no harm done. In fact, I dare say I am enjoying her company as well as the rest of your family. They are nowhere near as cold as their eldest daughter," Rhyes remarked, taking her boldly by the waist, hefting her unceremoniously up onto her mount.

"I beg your pardon?" Jocelyn asked, urging the beast forward when the shock of his words had worn away, leaving her to realize she was staring dumbfounded at his back as he was riding toward the gate.

"Was I not clear?" Rhyes asked when she was riding beside him. "You are cold, your kin are not."

"I most certainly am not," Jocelyn gasped, shocked to the very core with his blunt statement.

"There is no reason for anger I am only making an observation. Your kin are hospitable and charming, when you, on the other hand, are cold and distant. Are you certain you are related?"

"You Sir, are the most horrid of all men I have ever encountered. How dare you speak to me in such a way? You know nothing of me.

"It is only for the reason that I do not trust you that I keep my distance. Perhaps I know you better than my family, perhaps this is the only reason they are swept up in your charm."

"So you admit you find me charming?" Rhyes inquired as the party ahead of them entered the seclusion of the forest.

"Nay…I find you cunning and…and—"

"Charming," Rhyes supplied when it seemed she no longer had a mind to think for herself.

Rhyes only smiled at her scowl and offered her a playful wink.

Jocelyn put heel to her mount and pulled ahead of him, disappearing into the trees along with the others.

He knew he was irritating her beyond all reason, but there was something to be said for that. He was certain she wouldn't be so annoyed with him flirting with her sister if she didn't care even the slightest bit for him.

Jocelyn was a stubborn woman, he would give her that, but he was a patient man. He had no problem waiting about until she gave into his will and became his bride.

Later the same night, Jocelyn stood alone on the battlements, her eyes fixed on the sun as it slowly drowned behind the distant mountains.

She chewed absently on her bottom lip, contemplating if it was time she stepped up and bid Sir Rhyes farewell.

He'd been at Artois for well on a month now, there was no reason why he couldn't be on his way.

"Jocelyn?" her father's voice came from behind, startling her slightly. "Tomas told me I might find you here."

"Good evening, father," she greeted, lacing her arm through his when he came to stand beside her.

"I have not had a moment alone with you since we arrived," Robin commented, his eyes following hers to the distance.

"Have you dark secrets to tell me?" Jocelyn asked, fearing he'd come to discover the reason she insisted upon hiding.

"Nay love, but I would like for nothing more than to have you confide in me. I have spoken to Tomas concerning the last handful of months, he told me you have had an army of visitors reside within the walls of Artois."

"What else has he told you?" she asked, hoping there would be nothing left to tell.

"That you are not yourself. He is worried about you, as I am." Robin silently watched her for a moment. He could sense her anxiety and frustration and couldn't help but feel some responsibility for it.

"Would you wish to know who is to blame for your recent onslaught of suitors?" Robin questioned, gaining her full attention.

Her green eyes searched his face, seeming to know the answer to his question simply by the tone of his voice.

"You?" Jocelyn gasped in shock.

"I bid the first dozen or so men to seek a different path before I realized it was not my place to decide your future.

"You are the Lady of Artois; you need not your father blazing your path. The next throng I told just that, that you would decide your future, not I. I fear I should have warned you before I sent an army of men pounding down your door.

"Will you forgive me?" Robin asked, as twilight settled in around them.

In truth, it wasn't her father's fault that brought her unhappiness, namely if he was willing to give her the ability to choose for herself the man she would marry. It was a blessing, not a horrid sentence that would condemn her to a life of sorrow bound to a man she despised.

"I might have been happy once," Jocelyn whispered before she could stop herself, then fell silent hoping he didn't hear the soft confession.

"Aye, but it was not meant to be. None can change the past, we must only learn to live through it," Robin tenderly counseled.

Jocelyn nodded then shook back her tears, knowing there was no point in clinging to that which was lost.

She couldn't bring Bart back into her life.

Her heart would truly mend and then perhaps she could allow one of these men into her heart.

"What of Sir Rhyes?" Robin asked when torches were lit in the yard below, flicking against the night as a dozen fireflies determined to light the crushing darkness.

"What of him?"

"He seems a good man," Robin pushed, longing to know what his daughter thought of him.

"Many a man is not what he seems," Jocelyn supplied, folding her arms against the chill of the night air.

"Is Sir Rhyes not what he seems?" Robin questioned, turning to face her.

"I know not what he is. I only know that I do not fully trust him. Has Tomas not told you about him?" she asked, studying his face in the dim light.

She knew not if it was the darkness that caused him to look older to her eyes, or if it was his concern for her, but there was no denying that her father was changed, just as everything else in her life was changing.

"Tomas said little regarding the man, though he has expressed his concern for you," Robin replied, longing for Jocelyn to let go of all that troubled her and live with the spark of happiness that filled her life only years ago.

Jocelyn nodded with his words and looked back to the yard below.

"You would welcome Rhyes as my husband?" Jocelyn questioned, not daring to look at him then.

She feared he would see the truth in her eyes and press her further to be the woman she was before the man who held her heart died in her arms.

She needed yet more time, but if her father chose to push her to marry, then she would not refuse him.

Robin seemed to think, as everyone else around her, that it was time she took a husband and settled into life.

"I would welcome any man who would make *you* happy," Robin assured her, placing a hand on her back as he spoke. "You were once the merriest of girls I ever beheld. Always were you strong, but behind that strength was a joyful and kindhearted woman who was ever willing to love those around her. I know not what has become of the woman you once were, but I know you will never find happiness with any man until you remember who you are."

"What am I other than the heiress of Artois?" she asked, her voice laced with disdain.

“You are so much more, love. There is no sense in longing for happiness if you are lost in despair. Pull yourself up and make the life you long to live happen. No one can do this but you.” Robin kissed her on the cheek then left her to her own reflections.

Jocelyn stood on the battlements for a good part of the evening, looking to the horizon and feeling as though there was a part of her life that was missing, a part of her life her soul was still longing to live in spite of her sorrow.

Chapter Five

Tristan of Summerly looked upon the weathered face of his father, certain what he was asking was foolish, even as his loyalty to the man was forcing him to consider what Mortan was begging him to do.

"Why not send a missive to the lady and invite her to Summerly? Surely she would love nothing more than to come," Tristan suggested to the wild shaking of his father's head.

"Nay!" Mortan bellowed.

His son did not understand, just as Mortan feared he wouldn't.

"You must bring her here!" Mortan demanded even though he feared his son would never truly listen.

The long ride to Summerly had worn on his resolve, chipping away at his reason until there was little left to sustain him.

The only thought that consumed Mortan now was that Jocelyn must be brought to him, she must help him before it was too late.

"By force?" Tristan asked, squinting his pale green eyes at his father when the man continued to briskly shake his head.

"I care not how you manage to bring her here, only that you must. She must come to Summerly, she must know, she must!" Mortan rested his head in his hands, bringing his son to the foot of his chair with his sudden outburst of emotion.

"Father, you are unwell. Allow me to summon the healer," Tristan breathed, placing a hand on the man's trembling shoulder.

"You must bring her here…I must speak with her," Mortan wheezed, his voice overrun with emotion.

They were running out of time.

The longer his son sat on his heels the more time Rhyes had to entice the lady. She would give sway to his wishes, Mortan was certain of it. They must make haste.

"Aye father," Tristan finally agreed and stood, leery to leave the man alone for fear he wasn't well.

Mortan returned from Artois a week past and had never once ceased in speaking of the fair lady he'd resided with.

Tristan feared his father was losing what little sense was left to him.

Never had Tristan seen him thus.

Tristan left his father's chamber, coming face to face with his aunt who looked equally as concerned for her brother as was his son.

“He is not himself,” Mona murmured, tucking a graying strand of hair beneath her crisp wimple.

“Nay,” Tristan agreed, glancing back at the door behind him.

If his father was so distraught, he could do nothing but try his best to help him, even if that meant traveling to Artois to beg the grand lady to answer his father’s wishes.

“Perhaps I should send for the healer?” Mona asked more to herself than to Tristan who was already a good way down the corridor and nearly to the stairs.

“Would you have me send for the healer?” she called after him.

“Do what you must. I am to Artois, I will return in haste.” With that, Tristan was gone, leaving Mona to fend for herself.

Mona stood wringing her hands in the corridor, worrying over what should be done to help her brother.

When her fretting gained her nothing but further anxiety she reached out and tapped lightly upon the rough wood of the door before pushing it open to gaze at the withered figure of her bother.

Mortan sat in his large chair by the hearth, looking bent and broken. It caused Mona’s heart to ache with the mere sight of him. Never before had he looked so aged.

“Might I send for the healer?” Mona asked, taking another step into the chamber. She only longed to help him.

“Fetch Doyle to me,” Mortan mumbled, his voice so rough and low she barely heard it.

“What, brother?” Mona asked, entering the room more fully.

“Doyle!” Mortan bellowed so abruptly she stumbled backward.

“Nay, brother. You swore you would never use his services again, not after the last time,” she pleaded, but knew he would never yield, not when his eyes held such fire.

It was Mortan alone who brought their ruin upon them, employing such men as Doyle and his army of ruffians.

“Fetch him woman or you will no longer have a roof over your head!” Mortan threatened, gaining his feet. “Bring him! Bring him!” he bellowed as she fled the room, his voice pounding in her ears as she scurried down the corridor in search of a messenger.

Near three days later Doyle and his men rode through the gates of Summerly, their menacing presence pounding fear into Mona’s heart.

Doyle was more than happy to answer a summons that had always paid very well in the past.

Her brother was a fool.

Mona ushered her nieces upstairs to the lady’s solar and bolted the door, determined to remain locked away until the mercenaries were no longer within the walls of her home.

Mortan was asking for his death by bringing the blaggard here. She knew her brother had not the means to pay him. There was nothing left to the keep, her brother owed more than he could ever pay.

Once his creditors began calling in their debt, they would be ruined.

Mortan looked to the menacing, black haired man before him as any worthy saint would look to salvation.

This man was his last hope.

He'd sent Tristan to bring her to Summerly, but what if she refused him? What if her family refused to allow her to leave?

"You summoned, my Lord?" Doyle asked more than ready to get on with business.

"I have a task for you, if you are willing."

"I am ever willing if the price is right, you of all should know as much, or you would not have sent for me," Doyle remarked, resting his hand leisurely on the hilt of his blade as he spoke.

"Travel to Artois and see that my son is successful in freeing the lady of her obligations. He is to bring her to Summerly with all haste. I know her family is within residence and I want nothing to hinder him. I want no one to pursue them." Mortan looked to the man with all hope, knowing if his wishes were to come to pass this would be the man to see it happen.

"You trust not your son?" Doyle questioned, wondering what Mortan was thinking to attempt to kidnap such a lady.

Had the old fool finally lost his mind?

"I trust not those who reside with her. They will keep her there; they will not allow her to leave. She must, and you must see it happen," Mortan ordered, pushing unsteadily to his feet, his eyes filled with wild desperation.

"I will make it worth your while. Have I not always made it worth your while?"

Doyle nodded his agreement and turned to fetch his men.

The lady of Artois was a rich prize indeed. There was no doubt in his mind that Mortan would pay highly to have such a trophy safely delivered. Should the blundering man forget, Doyle would take the prize for himself.

Doyle knew what a ransom would be on such a lady, he would rest in luxury for the rest of his days and that was incentive enough for him to turn in the direction of Artois and ride as though the devil was nipping at his heels.

"Not while your father is within the keep," Tomas answered, pushing past Jocelyn to make his way to the lists.

"He will never know," Jocelyn pleaded, running after him, determined to have his compliance.

"He will know, Jo, for I will tell him."

"Are you still angry with me?" Jocelyn asked when Tomas came to a stop and bellowed for his squire.

"I am not angry with you and I will not take you out to hunt upon the morrow." Tomas shrugged his heavy mailed shirt on over his head with the aid of his squire then began fastening his thick belt about his waist.

"Who is your master he or I?" Jocelyn questioned, knowing if his mind was made up she would never sway him.

"He…it is time you found your own captain, Jo. I cannot always remain here with you. My home is at Milberk, serving your father." Tomas took his sword from his squire and turned from her, ready to enter the lists and practice his skill.

"You are angry with me still." Jocelyn frowned at him when Tomas turned back to face her.

His pale blue eyes were so dark she barely recognized them. Never had she seen him so frustrated.

"Nay, I am angry with the choices you have made of late, not with you," Tomas answered, pulling at his gloves, with a heightened sense of aggression.

"Is that not the same?" she inquired, aggravated with the rift that was growing between them.

Tomas was her friend and had been since they were both a good deal younger, well before he was her father's captain.

"I am sorry for the offences I have caused you, but I know not what I can do to mend them. What would you have me do?" Jocelyn asked when he was ready to leave her.

"Send him packing," Tomas hissed when Rhyes dark head appeared in the distance.

"He is not for you. I know one day you must marry, but I will die before it is to a man such as him. He does not belong here, Jo." With that,

Tomas turned and left her, making his way into the lists to attack his opponent with intensified hostility.

Jocelyn turned on her heel and stalked across the yard to where Rhyes was approaching her, bent on sending him on his way. But, before she could utter a word, he lifted his hand, presenting her with a small yellow flower.

"Truce" Rhyes offered, smiling gallantly at her. "I am weary of you loathing me."

Jocelyn took a breath and accepted the offering, her heart slightly smoothed over with the gesture.

"Then you are sorry for accusing me of being cold?" she questioned, hating the way his remark made her feel.

"I am, if you have a mind to prove me otherwise."

"How so?" Jocelyn tipped her head at him, wondering how she might do such a thing.

"I know not, walk with me a while. Speak with me without your judgment getting in the way of the conversation. Truly, I am a good man." Rhyes offered her his arm, then stood patiently waiting for her to accept.

"I know not, Sir."

She thought of Tomas, his anger toward this man and considered returning to the keep. Alas, her feet remained planted in the yard.

"I swear, you will suffer no ill from me," he vowed looking her square in the eyes as he spoke.

"Very well," Jocelyn sighed, accepting his offered arm, allowing him to lead her in the direction of the gardens.

For a brief moment she glanced over her shoulder to the lists, her eyes catching sight of Tomas where he stood looking at her, his sword lowered, his pale eyes filled with deep betrayal.

How could she be so torn? She longed to please Tomas, just as she valued his friendship. Even so, this man who led her now intrigued her.

Certainly there must be a reason.

"Your father has made the comment to me that you are in need of a captain of your own," Rhyes remarked, pulling her attention back to him.

"One day I will need to seek out one of my own, as of now I trust Tomas. I am—Artois is well looked after with him here," she answered.

The conversation she had only just had with Tomas filled her mind, causing her brow to furrow in question. Tomas spoke similar words to her only moments ago. Was he truly thinking of leaving Artois?

"I do not wish to speak of this now," Jocelyn informed him, too frustrated with the thought to linger on it.

"Very well, what would you have us speak of?" Rhyes asked, his voice smooth and easy.

"Have you nothing to occupy your life, Sir?" she questioned, pulling her arm from his to face him.

What sort of man was he to loiter at her home for so long?

He seemed not to have a care in the world other than tormenting her.

"Nay, I am here because of you. Do you not remember?" Rhyes gave her a smile that warmed her flesh though her stubborn will refused to accept it.

"Then I would ask you to leave, for I am not ready to accept you," Jocelyn stated firmly, hoping he would take her words to heart and pursue her no longer.

"I have offered you nothing," Rhyes remarked, causing her blood to heat.

"You have implied plenty…you cannot stay here," Jocelyn stated, shaking her head at him.

She turned from Rhyes, ready to make her way back to the keep and leave their conversation at that. She'd bid him leave, perhaps now Tomas would no longer despise her.

"Why have you shut your heart away?" Rhyes asked, bringing her feet to an unwilling halt.

"I have done no such thing," she defended, turning to gape at him in defense.

"Aye, but you have. Was it a man perhaps? Did he cast you aside and give his love to another?" Rhyes bit his tongue when he realized his teasing words cut far deeper than he intended.

Jocelyn stood staring at him wide-eyed and pale, biting her lower lip as though it would take away the deep sting of his comment.

"Forgive me, Jocelyn, I only assumed," Rhyes said, though he knew the damage was already done.

"I…I loved him," she whispered after a moment of silence. "I loved him with all my heart and he desired my dear cousin. Had I not loved Meredith as a sister, I would have despised her. I saw him nearly every day of my life, yet he knew not that I lived.

"Not until the moment when he took his last breath did he truly see me. Not until he lay dying in *my* arms did he realize I lived for him." Jocelyn numbly shook her head at Rhyes with her solemn confession, her heart breaking anew with the vivid memories of that day.

"Men are a thickheaded lot," Rhyes stated, knowing not how to comfort her. He knew not how any man could look at her and not truly see her.

"Aye, as are women." Jocelyn wiped at her eyes, slightly embarrassed with the tears that seemed to escape without her realizing it.

"I long for happiness, I long for what my mother has with my father. But, I fear that for the now, my heart is still lost to another.

"I am not cold as you think me to be, or aloof as the other men surely know me to be. I am not ready to love again. I fear I am too afraid to lose," Jocelyn solemnly confessed.

"More than that, I refuse to be used for the gain of another," she scolded.

"How will you ever gain if you do not allow your heart to open?" Rhyes asked, reaching out to take her hand.

"How will I live if I am forced to suffer the loss of losing all my heart has ever longed for?"

"Touché." Rhyes kissed her hand briefly, then tipped his head at her tear-streaked face. "I was mistaken…you are far from cold. You are, in fact, the vast opposite.

"I am glad you allowed me to remain in your company long enough to be witness to it. I cannot go against your wishes. I will leave at first light and hinder you no more." Rhyes released her hand and took a step back.

He offered her a low bow and left her where she stood, regretting her decision to send him on his way.

Perhaps there was more to this man than met the eye.

Chapter Six

Rhyes checked his mount one final time before glancing to the keep.

There was still a good hour before the sun would bid him good day and he wanted to be well from the walls before he was forced to explain his dismissal to her kin.

Jocelyn bid him leave and that was what he must do.

Rhyes could see himself as master of this place. He could also see himself forever with Jocelyn, but he would give her the time her heart needed. For now, he had no choice in the matter.

Rhyes was truly beginning to care for her and because of this; he could not press her as all the others had.

Now that he knew the reasons behind her distance, he felt as though he could safely step back and allow Jocelyn the time she required to find herself.

He would win her. He had no doubt that one day Jocelyn would be his wife.

Rhyes looked to his men; they were all mounted and ready to depart. It was a small party to be sure, but he was certain that one day he would have a garrison to match Lord Milberk's.

It was then that Rhyes noticed Jocelyn descending the stairs of the keep.

She was dressed again in the tunic and hose of a man, her hair tucked up under a cap. A knife and sword strapped to her slender waist.

He smiled with the sight of her. At first glance, she looked like nothing more than a squire, off to morning chores.

"Sir," Jocelyn called out, ensuring she'd gained his attention.

"Good morrow, Lady. As you see I am good to my word. I will leave you in peace," Rhyes assured, offering her a slight bow when she came to stand before him.

"I cannot, in good conscience, let you go," Jocelyn informed him, her cheeks turning crimson against her will when she spoke.

"I spoke out of sorts and I am sorry. You may stay if you wish it, or you may leave if you so desire. I only wish to tell you that I was mistaken."

"You wish me to stay?" Rhyes asked, wondering if he looked as stunned as he felt.

"I know not what I wish. I only know I might come to regret your leaving." Jocelyn sighed and took a mighty breath before continuing.

"My father speaks highly of you, yet my dear friend despises you. My poor heart is in turmoil and my mind can no longer think for itself.

"I know not why you should leave when we are just beginning to know one another."

Rhyes nodded with her words, noting she looked more than a little fatigued.

"You look exhausted," he observed out loud, clearly taking notice of her brisk irritation with his observation.

"I was afraid to sleep for fear I would sleep through your departure and not be allowed to mend things between us," Jocelyn confessed, shifting from foot to foot as she spoke.

"Awe, Lady, you lost sleep over me," Rhyes beamed, truly touched with her concern.

"Nay, it was my conscience that kept me from sleeping," Jocelyn snapped, hoping he wouldn't force her to regret stopping him.

"I see no difference," Rhyes gloated, puffing his chest out slightly as he spoke.

It was good to know she was thinking of him, even in the slightest way.

"It is far too early to quarrel with you, Sir." Jocelyn gave him a glare and looked past him to the stables, clearly ready to be on her way.

"Fair enough...but I am flattered none-the-less. I cannot help but notice that you look ready for the hunt. Do you ride out with Tomas?" he asked, tipping his head at her when she glanced at him.

There was no doubt his winning the lady would be far easier if her dear captain was out of the way.

The man was positively irritating, always looking on whenever Rhyes found a quiet moment with Jocelyn, no doubt ready to offer his opinion of her guest with little care for offence.

"Nay, he refuses to take me while my father is within the walls. I thought to seek out the master huntsman and persuade him to take me. Though I would rather go with Tomas…the coward," Jocelyn mumbled, again looking around Rhyes to the stables.

"Allow me to take you," Rhyes suggested, more than willing to take her out.

He knew she enjoyed the solitude of the hunt. She was not one to bring along the dogs or a throng of men, she preferred the quiet and in her company he would as well.

Jocelyn studied him for a moment then looked to the dim hue of the sky. If they were to go, it would have to be soon.

"You fear not my father's wrath?" Jocelyn asked after a prolonged moment of silence.

"I fear him, Lady, but for you it is a risk I will take. Come, you may have my mount and I will take one of my men's as to not hinder us further," Rhyes suggested, ready to help her up onto the saddle.

They would be back well before any found them missing, he had no fear of Robin loathing him for seeing to the safety of his daughter.

"Very well," Jocelyn agreed allowing him to help her up onto his mount, then waited until he was ready before urging the beast forward.

Never once did she look back as they rode through the gates, neither did she listen to the quiet warning flitting through the brisk morning air.

Jocelyn longed for time outside the walls of her home and she needed to get to know this man in truth, without the hindering of those about her.

Tomas made his rounds about the battlements just as the sun rose above the distant trees.

His mind refused to be quieted, as images of Jocelyn standing with her arm draped over Sir Rhyes flooded his mind's eye.

Tomas despised the man, there was no denying it, but he could not place his finger on why.

He'd been witness to many a man's attempt to woo her. He'd been witness to it, but perhaps he never felt as though there would be anything gained by it.

Sir Rhyes was different from all the others; he was smooth and confident in a way that caused Tomas to squirm.

Tomas himself cared for Jocelyn, he'd cared for her for longer than he could remember, but deep within his soul he knew nothing would come of it. Tomas knew he would have to see her wed to another. Because of this, he made a vow to himself that he would see it was a good man who took the woman he loved to wife and not one who desired only her wealth.

Still, Tomas struggled to believe Rhyes was a good man, or was it the simple fact that he found it hard to believe that any man, but he, was able to love Jocelyn and look after her as he could?

Tomas finished his rounds before making his way to the hall to break his fast.

Lord Milberk and his lady wife, as well as Liza sat at the grand table, merrily conversing with one another, but Jocelyn and the offensive Rhyes were nowhere to be found.

"Good morrow, Tomas," Robin greeted, motioning for the man to approach. "Come, join us my friend."

Tomas made himself comfortable at the high table, loading his plate with the offered fare. He'd never been the sort of man to pass up a good meal.

"I have a mind to ride out after we have finished our meal. I would like to see how my daughter is managing her holding," Robin informed him, before taking a drink from his goblet.

"Might I go with you father?" Liza asked, her face lit with hope.

"I see no reason why you cannot. Fetch your sister, will you? I would like her to know of my plans should she wish to go along as well." Robin nodded for Liza to leave only to be startled by her reply.

"Jocelyn left early this morning," Liza supplied, brushing her hair back from her face as she spoke.

"Left?" Sarah questioned. Looking at her from where she sat beside her husband.

"Aye, her maid said she left to make certain Sir Rhyes didn't leave as she bid him to. She told me he was to leave this morning at Jocelyn's request. Jo must have had a change of heart.

"I know not why she would ever think of sending him away. Rhyes is a most handsome of men. Why, I myself think him to be wonderful," Liza mooned, hugging her shoulders as she spoke.

"Perhaps that is why your opinion of the man has never been asked," Tomas muttered, standing briskly to make for the door.

Rhyes' men were still within residence, so the lout must still be here as well.

"Tomas, where go you?" Robin was following after him, his eyes brimmed with concern.

"Jocelyn asked me yesterday to take her out on a private hunt this morning. I denied her, shortly after that I saw her conversing with Rhyes. I have a feeling the lout has stepped up where I backed down." He bounded down the stairs and made to the stables.

He was determined to track them down before Rhyes could use his cunning to break his way into Jocelyn's heart.

"Jocelyn would not be so foolish as to ride out without the huntsman," Robin assured Tomas as they entered the stables.

"Aye, my Lord," the huntsman called out upon hearing his name.

The huntsman was sitting on a low stool in the corner, seeing to an assortment of weapons.

Robin turned back to Tomas, his eyes filled with questions.

"I have taken her out many a time," Tomas confessed, before calling orders for his horse to be saddled as well as Robin's.

"Alone?" Robin asked, his temper beginning to flair.

Robin had told Jocelyn more times than he could count of the dangers of the hunt. It was not safe go out without the aid of the huntsman and his men. They were there for a reason. If she was so foolish as to overlook their purpose, then she was too foolish to take on the sport.

"Aye. There has never been a cause for alarm, my Lord. I am enough to look after her. She has never come to harm under my watch." Tomas mounted his horse and turned to the gates, Robin pounding along beside him.

"I sent you with her to Artois to look after her, not to indulge her and endanger her life. I never thought you to be so reckless." Robin's anger with his captain nearly consumed him as they passed through the gate and made for the woods.

How could Tomas be so foolish as to allow Jocelyn to believe she needed no more protection than one man?

They dug in their heels, urging the horses to eat up the ground beneath them.

The moment they entered the woods, they were forced to slow the animals to a pace that would insure they caught sight of the pair they sought.

Tomas felt the thickness in the air around him, the silence in the stead of the many noises that should be taking place in the crisp morning air.

Every fiber of his being told him something was not as it should be.

Something was terribly wrong.

Doyle crouched down in the long grass, watching, ever so patiently, as the woman in the distance lifted her bow and took aim at a boar wallowing in a nearby mud hole.

She was alone save for one man who was keeping a close watch over her every move. The hand of her guard was resting on the hilt of his sword, as he sensed something the lady was missing. The man seemed to know they were being watched, but he said nothing to her concerning it, keeping a silent watch as she enjoyed her sport.

Doyle's men were set at intervals throughout the forest and were ready to do as their master bid them.

Tristan, Lord Summerly's son, was not but two miles away where he'd passed the night in a clearing. The camp was in motion, ready to break their rest and make way to Artois.

Doyle and his men would have no trouble freeing the lady of her guard and sending her neatly in Tristan's direction.

He was certain the heir of Summerly could take it from there. It would then be up to Doyle and his men to see Tristan and the woman weren't followed.

Doyle lifted his crossbow, aiming the weapon at the man who rode beside Lady Artois and then he waited until the moment was right.

Jocelyn held her breath, honing in on the animal in the distance. Her eyes were intently fixed on the beast as he unknowingly endangered his life by heedlessly wallowing in the mud.

She took a final breath and released, striking the boar in the flesh of his neck sending him to the mud.

Jocelyn turned to beam at Sir Rhyes just as an arrow came out of nowhere. It struck him in the shoulder with such force it sent Rhyes careening to the ground.

"Rhyes!" she screamed, ready to dismount and help him when a thunder of shouts and hooves rose up in the concealment of the trees around them.

"Back to the keep!" Rhyes ordered from where he was gaining his feet.

"I will not leave you," Jocelyn argued, watching him pull the arrow from his shoulder with an agonizing yell.

Rhyes cast the offending arrow aside and took hold of his sword ready to defend her.

"You will!" With the blunt edge of his weapon, Rhyes smacked her mount on his hindquarters, sending the beast tearing off in the direction of Artois.

Jocelyn gripped the reins, struggling to gain even the slightest bit of control as three men appeared through the trees before her, giving the horse no choice, but to turn away from the keep and plunge deeper into the forest.

She bent low over the head of her mount, clinging to the panicked animal with every ounce of her being.

The men were gaining on her, shouting and cursing as they gave chase, frightening the already frantic horse until there was no hope for Jocelyn to calm him.

Her cap flew from her head, when she glanced over her shoulder to find that much to her shock they were suddenly gone, pulling back to no longer give chase.

Jocelyn swallowed her terror and struggled to gain her bearings as the trees and boulders flew by at a reckless pace.

She pulled back on the reins, only to gain no response from the frightened beast.

Just then, the men were back, this time coming from the left of her mount, turning the animal again, forcing the beast yet deeper into the forest.

She dug her heels in and forced the frothing animal forward, determined to gain just enough lead that she might point them in the direction of Artois.

If she could get closer to the keep there was a chance her peril would be discovered. As long as she was lost to the depths of the forest, there was little hope.

Tristan mounted his horse and took the reins from his squire. He was far from ready to make his way to Artois and beg the lady to accompany him to Summerly. In truth, he'd spent a good part of the night going over the mornings events in his mind, there were only two possible outcomes.

She would either be as her father described her and accompany him with little question, or she would throw him from her gates and he would be forced to return to Summerly without her.

None of this made any sense to him. Why would his father send him to fetch the lady? Why was he so adamant that she make the journey to Summerly?

Tristan shook his head and found himself contemplating the fact that his father might truly be on the verge of losing what was left of his wits.

He knew Mortan had not been himself for some time now, but this request was the worst of it. Yet, here he sat, ready to fulfill his father's wishes.

Perhaps it was the least he could do for the man who raised him. They were once very close, but of late, things were different, his father was distant and brooding. Mortan seemed to be struggling with some unknown burden, though he would not allow anyone to help him.

Tristan was ready to give the order for the small group of men to mount up so they might be on their way when a lone rider went tearing by in the distance.

He squinted at the image, then blinked a time or two wondering if his eyes were seeing falsely or if it was in fact a woman riding through the trees as though she was being pursued by some hideous beast.

It took him very little time to take in the wide-eyed, frothing horse she rode to guess that the wench had lost control of the beast and was in need of assistance.

Tristan turned his mount in the direction she'd gone and pushed the horse forward at a reckless speed. He hoped to catch the woman before she lost full control over the animal and found herself hurt or worse.

She glanced only once over her shoulder, her eyes full of fear when she took in the sight of him.

Tristan was ready to call out to her, to tell her that he meant no harm, but before he could utter a word, her horse jumped a shallow stream causing her to lose the hold she had on him and go flailing to the ground.

The animal continued to bolt, hardly caring that he was now riderless.

Tristan slowed his mount, dismounted and waded through the water to come to a stop on the opposite side of the stream where the woman lay on the bank, unconscious, but breathing.

"Fool wench," Tristan muttered under his breath and brushed a bit of the mud from her cheek, just as the unmistakable sound of riders filled his ears.

"Orders, my Lord?" Lance called out upon reaching him, his eyes fixed on the woman lying in the mud.

"Go after her mount, will you?" Tristan answered, receiving a hardy nod from his squire before the lad pounded away.

Tristan patted the woman's cheek attempting to rouse her, but she seemed heedless of his tapping for her eyes remained closed.

"I know her," one of his father's men offered, dismounting to get a better look at the woman.

"You know her?" Tristan questioned, looking to the man when he crouched down beside him.

"Aye. She is the Lady of Artois," he stated, looking nearly as stunned as his master.

"This sad, bedraggled urchin is the grand Lady my father sent me to fetch?" Tristan asked, hardly willing to believe that she'd simply fallen into their hands.

"I swear it. I saw her dressed in such a way when she rode out to hunt. I am not mistaken, I give you my word."

Tristan sat back on his heels, contemplating the choice that was now placed before him.

He could take her back to Artois. Or, as she was not in the place to decide for herself, he could cart her along to Summerly. By the time she awoke, she would be so far from home she would surely continue on the rest of the way without dispute.

Tristan pushed to his feet and shook his head at the poor wench.

When he thought of a woman as grand as the Lady of Artois, this pitiable looking thing was far from what he pictured. None-the-less, if his father wished to see her, then he would see it come to pass.

Tomas pulled his mount to a halt when a sight that might have, at one time, caused him to rejoice filled his sight.

Rhyes lay on the trampled ground, bleeding from a deep wound in his shoulder and another on his brow.

He dismounted to the unmistakable sound of Robin drawing his sword and crouch down by the man to see if he still lived.

"Rhyes?" Tomas shook the man roughly, managing to gain his attention at last. "What happened? Where is Jocelyn?"

"There are men in the wood—" Rhyes managed before shaking off his delirium and struggled to gain his feet. "I sent her back to the keep." His eyes then fell to where Robin sat upon his horse looking down on him in disappointed rage.

"She was riding toward Artois, and well, when last I saw her," Rhyes vowed, knowing if she was not, it would be his doing.

"Back to the keep," Robin ordered, his heart thumping so wildly he knew not if he would ever again be able to breathe without struggling for air.

A handful of moments later, they passed through the gates and came to a stop in the yard where Sarah and Liza were waiting, though much to the horror of all three of the men, Jocelyn was not to be seen.

"What happened?" Sarah questioned, running to stand at her husband's stirrup.

"Pray tell me she is here," Robin begged, but instantly knew his answer for his wife's face turned deathly white.

"Nay…Robin what happened?" Sarah asked again, her eyes pleading with him for answers.

"She rode out with this fool of a man!" Tomas shouted as he dismounted, stalked to where Rhyes sat on the back of his mount, boldly reached up and yanked the injured man to the ground to punch him soundly across the face.

Rhyes instantly returned the abuse, sending the fuming Tomas to his backside.

"I only did what I have seen *you* do a number of times. She wished to ride out, I merely obliged her!" Rhyes argued, shaking his hand when it burned from striking Tomas down.

"Do not blame this on Jocelyn!" Tomas shouted, gaining his feet to pull his sword from its sheath. "If she had been with me, she would still be here. It was you who did not protect her and now she is gone!"

Rhyes had no choice, but to draw his weapon and defend himself as Tomas attacked him with blow after blow. His pride and honor marred by the words of his foe.

Rhyes knew he hadn't been enough to protect her and now she was lost. He would bring her back. Rhyes vowed he would, but first he must rid himself of the passionate captain.

"Enough!" Robin ordered, his anger with their dispute fueled by his daughter's disappearance.

He dismounted and ran to where the men were locked in combat, seemingly determined to end the other's life before the morning was over.

Robin had nearly succeeded in separating the fools when the warning call of approaching riders was bellowed from the wall.

That chilling sound alone was enough to silence their fighting, bringing them all together to the wall to climb the stairs to see for themselves if it was friend or foe approaching the keep.

As they looked out over the distance, the fear of the inevitable smothered any chance there had once been for hope; they took in the sight of an army of men advancing on Artois.

They wore no identifying colors over their mailed shirts and sported no banners to tell their enemy whom they served. The sight of the group brought with them the thick, menacing presence of evil.

"Close the gate!" Robin bellowed, his anger rising up anew, he had a feeling this advancing group had everything to do with his missing daughter.

"Man the wall…to the battlements!"

"Look what you have done!" Tomas sneered at Rhyes who only pushed past the fuming captain and stalked to the yard below.

Rhyes needed to bandage his shoulder and head, as well as ready his men for the inevitable. More importantly, he needed to try to contain his blistering temper before he angered Robin further by removing the irksome captain of his life.

Chapter Seven

Jocelyn felt the warmth of a crackling fire and slowly became aware of the conversing of low voices in the distance.

Her body ached, her head pounded and she had to think for a moment to remind herself of why she felt as she did.

She'd been hunting with Rhyes, she killed the boar and then—

Jocelyn sat up bolt straight as the images of Rhyes being shot and the men who thundered after her burst into her thoughts.

"Easy there…" a man's voice warned as her head spun and her vision blurred. "You might want to take it slow for a while. You have quite the bump on the head, but I dare say everything else is sound."

His face slowly began to come into focus before her, the smiling weather-worn face of a man who looked, that more often than not, as though he spent his days in merry contentment. The soft smile lines around his eyes and mouth spoke of a man who seemed to find joy in his life.

His hair was cropped short to his head and of a sandy brown color. She could not tell his height from where he crouched down before her, but judged from his broad, toned shoulders that he didn't take his time in the lists for granted.

"There you see, that's better. Your head does not pound so much when you have a care."

He sat down across the fire when it seemed she was well enough to sit up on her own and commenced in finishing his evening meal.

Jocelyn took in the fire-lit darkness around her, counting three other fires and a cluster of men around each of them.

She could clearly hear the whinny of horses and the gentle babble of a nearby stream. Then much to her alarm, she noticed the canopy of the forest was gone, giving way to the blanket of stars that winked down from the heavens above.

"Where am I?" Jocelyn asked when it seemed he had no intentions of speaking to her further.

"I would say somewhere between here and there. Are you hungry?" he asked, standing to make his way across camp.

Jocelyn reached for the sword she wore on her belt irritated to find it missing as well as her hunting knife.

The man stopped for a moment at one of the fires before returning to hand her a laden plate.

"Where are my weapons?" Jocelyn asked, refusing to accept his offering, though her stomach growled loud in protest.

"I found it strange for a woman to carry such a knife, but even more so a sword. I thought it best if they were removed from your person just in case you might know how to use them.

"Know you how to use them?" he inquired, clearly noticing that the question caused her blood to boil.

"Aye, I know how to use them!" she bellowed, longing to have the weapons in her possession at that moment to prove it to the twit.

"Remarkable," the man mused, resuming his place across from her, resting the laden plate at his side.

"What do you want from me?" Jocelyn asked after a moment of silent staring at one another.

"Nothing overly dramatic. My father fervently bid me to seek you out…it would seem he dearly wishes to see you again," he remarked, offering her the food a second time.

Jocelyn looked at him with a scowl, struggling to make sense of his words.

"Your father?"

"Aye, I knew not who you were until my man informed me. As I was sent to fetch you, I thought there would be no harm in bringing you with us. You surely wish to send a missive to your kin to let them know you are well. I thought to send one myself, but I feared they would think I meant you harm," he supplied, his smile never wavering.

"You tell me you mean me no harm, yet for all I know, you killed my escort and then ran me down in the woods! How is this bringing me no harm?" Jocelyn asked, her voice rising in anger.

The man's smile slowly faded as her words seemed to sink into his thick skull.

He eyed her for a moment before leaning forward to look at her intently.

"Tell me, Lady, why was your mount in such a panic?"

"I was being rundown by *your* men…what other reason would he have?" she ranted, her anger growing rapidly.

"It was not my men," he murmured, his eyes never leaving her face. "You say your escort was killed."

"He was shot with an arrow, he forced me to leave him. He thought I could make it back to the keep before we were overrun." Jocelyn studied his face in the firelight, noting something slightly familiar about his eyes though she couldn't place it.

He sat back and placed a hand over his mouth, as he quietly contemplated what she'd told him. Then he rose without warning and made his way into camp, bellowing for men as he went.

"The lady was overrun in the woods. I want three of you to return to Artois. Her family will surely think she is lost. I will take her on to Summerly. Make haste!" he ordered.

Jocelyn pushed to her feet with the realization of the man's identity. Her fear and anger faded away as she now knew she had nothing to fear from him.

"Tristan?" Jocelyn questioned, when he turned back to face her, clearly shocked to see her standing.

"Aye," Tristan answered, his mouth turning up in a smile.

"I know your father," she informed him, swaying slightly as the outer limits of her vision darkened, threatening to send her to the ground.

"That you do." Tristan crossed to her quickly and helped her to sit.

He crouched down before her, searching her face with his pale green eyes to be certain she was well.

"I fear he is not himself. He is asking for you, and as I am his only son, I could not help but fulfill his wishes, even if they were more than a little odd."

"He is ill?" Jocelyn whispered, saddened with the news.

"The man is well past his prime, I fear his mind and body are not as they once were. I know not why, but he was adamant about seeing you. He was home only a week and yet you were all he spoke of. Are you well?" Tristan asked once it seemed the haze that threatened to take her had passed.

"Aye, my thanks." Jocelyn watched him resume his place across from her, retrieve the plate of food he'd prepared and passed it to her.

Tristan smiled softly when she accepted the meal, seeming that they were no longer enemies, there was no reason to avoid his hospitality.

"Your father fell ill while he resided at Artois. I begged him to allow me to send for you, but he refused. To be truthful, there was something in his eyes when he left that caused me to worry for him. He seemed tired and distant and perhaps sad," Jocelyn remarked, taking a bite of the meat Tristan offered her.

"I fear he is a man that will not lightly accept the help of others," Tristan chuckled softly and rested his arms on his folded legs. "It has been years since he has truly been himself.

"I have offered many a time to take over the affairs of Summerly, but each time, he has pushed me away. I fear the task of seeing to so many has worn on him more than any can truly know."

"Why would he ask for me?" Jocelyn asked after a moment of listening to the fire crackle and pop against the night.

Tristan didn't answer her question for a moment, as he seemed to ponder her words carefully.

"I know not…I only know that I felt little choice but to grant his request. I fear he will not be with us much longer." Tristan paused for a moment, looking to her as though he was thinking over their strange situation.

"In good conscience, I cannot force you to travel with me to Summerly, my men are ready to depart. If you wish it you may go with them. They can return you with all haste to your kin."

Jocelyn quietly nodded at his offer.

Her good sense told her to return to Artois, but her need to answer Lord Summerly's request caused her to pull the simple silver ring from her finger and hold it out to him.

"Have your men give this to my father, it was a gift from him. He will know it is mine. Have them tell him I journey to Summerly to visit a most dear friend."

"I will see it done." Tristan took the trinket from her, stood and made his way quickly through the camp to where the men he was sending to Artois were making ready to leave.

Jocelyn had a deep nagging feeling that she should go with them, but if Lord Summerly was in some dire state, and asking for her, she feared she would regret not answering his request, namely if he was near the end of his life.

Mortan seemed to think he needed her and she couldn't help but wonder why.

It was the following evening when the three men Tristan sent to Artois approached Doyle's camp of mercenaries.

He'd laid siege to the keep and had succeeded in holding them at bay for the moment. He was to keep them from following after the woman and so he would.

"What news have you?" Doyle questioned the men when they were brought before him.

They knew all too well who he was, for their master had employed his services many times in the past.

"Is your Lord's son successful in swaying the lady to journey with him to Summerly?"

"Aye," was his only answer, giving Doyle cause to believe these men did not respect their lord's decision to employ his service.

"Very good. Have you a message from the lady?" Doyle asked, certain they would not return to Artois without word from the woman.

"Aye," the man sneered, his face flushed with anger as he extended his hand, offering Doyle a woman's silver ring. "Lord Milberk will know it is his daughter's."

The man then turned on his heel, taking with him his comrades, leaving Doyle to fume at the obvious disrespect.

"Go after them," Doyle ordered to the nearest man.

He would not be treated in such a way, not by anyone. He closed his hand over the ring as the clash of futile swords in the distance met his ears; it was only but a brief moment before it was again quiet.

He seemed to have the means now to demand a ransom of his own. He knew the honorable Lord Milberk would never forsake his daughter and as she was missing, Robin alone held control over the wealth of Artois.

Lord Summerly would never know. The man was too far-gone to know anything past his own delusions as it was.

He would allow Artois to wait it out for a awhile longer. Their worry would build so that when he placed his offer before them, there would be no refusing him.

Doyle turned to the massive keep, a sinister smile creeping across his weathered face.

Perhaps he would profit twice from his labors. There was no limit to the wealth one might gain with the proper amount of cunning.

"It was my grandmother's," Jocelyn informed him when Tristan inquired about her sword while they rode through the countryside.

"And you truly know how to use it, properly I mean?" Tristan asked, his voice edged with amusement.

"Aye, I know how to properly use it. Why would I wear if I knew not how to wield it?" Jocelyn shook her head at him.

The bright midmorning sun beat down upon their uncovered heads, granting them warmth and the comfort of easy travel.

"It is only remarkable. I have never known a woman who took the pains to dress as a man, strap a sword to her hip and proclaim to one and all that she was able to defend herself."

"It is not so remarkable within my family. Every woman knows her way with an array of weapons. My grandmother trained in the lists with her husband's own squire. My mother learned to fight alongside her brother and all of my kinswomen after them were trained in the art of battle.

"My younger sister cares not for the sport and would rather ply her needle, but if the need arose, she would carry her weight as well as any man." Jocelyn looked at him with pride as she defended her strange talent, hardly caring what Tristan thought of her. She was proud of who she was and where she hailed from.

"Does your sister dress as a man as well? For I must tell you I do prefer women dressed as women," Tristan remarked, a hint of jesting in his voice.

"I dress only as a man when I hunt. I see no reason to ruin a fine gown at the cost of sport," she informed him, feeling slightly self-conscious with the hose and tunic she was wearing.

"Awe, then you *are* a lady," Tristan teased, rubbing at his arm when she reached out and struck him.

"My apologies," he laughed, smiling widely at her. "Tell me, who was it that taught you how to fight and hunt and dress as a man?"

"I dress as a man on my own, Sir, and my father taught me to fight, with much persuasion from my mother. He would never have done so within my mother prodding."

"I can imagine a great lord such as the Lord of Artois would want nothing more for his daughter, than to see she was a refined young lady," Tristan suggested with a hardy nod.

"He is not the Lord of Artois, the man I call my father is Robin of Milberk. The Lord of Artois died well before I was born. I have been told he was a good and honorable man who loved my mother to a fault, just as he would have cherished me, but as I knew him not, I do not call him father.

"The only father I have ever known is the man who married my mother only months after I entered this life." Jocelyn paused and looked at him with a scowl, slightly concerned with how easy it was to converse with this man.

"I know not why I told you that. I fear I am rambling."

"Nay, sweet Lady. It is a part of who you are. I dare say I am intrigued. Robin of Milberk must be a fine man indeed to love another's child as dearly as his own," Tristan complimented.

"Aye, the finest I have ever known."

"You say you have sisters?" Tristan asked, noting a slight change in her countenance with the question.

She was the one who mentioned her family; she could not fault him for asking.

"Aye, Liza, who is with my family at Artois and Zoe who was taken from us only two years ago." She felt the same clinch of pain she felt when she thought of the horrid night.

Not only did she lose a most beloved sister, but an honorable man as well.

"I am sorry to hear it," Tristan offered, his low voice filled with earnest.

"It was a dark day…I have also a brother," Jocelyn rambled on, hoping to change the subject. "He is offering his services to Lord Norick, my mother's brother. He is very soon to win his spurs."

"That is well, a grand day in any man's life. I wish him all the very best." Tristan studied her face as he spoke.

She'd managed to change the subject in the blink of an eye, but the darkness that crossed her face with the mention of her sister was still there, hanging in the air above her as a threatening cloud ready to burst.

"Have you family other than your father?" Jocelyn inquired after a moment of quiet reflection. She knew of his sisters, yet she was greatly in the need of shifting the conversation to him.

"Five sisters, sweet Lady, all a good deal younger than myself. I adore them all, in moderation," he stated, laughing wholeheartedly when she looked at him in shocked question.

"They are constant. Their chatter is deafening, their squabbling inevitable and my love for them infinite. Alas, with so many women about, I dare say it is difficult for a man to survive. My aunt was kind enough to take residence in the keep after my mother passed; otherwise I know not how my father would manage."

"Your description of them reminds me of my sister, there are days when I know not where she sprung from," Jocelyn laughed, lightening his heart with the soft tones of her voice.

Tristan was beginning to see why his father would ask for her company. Jocelyn was a charming companion, not only was she sweet and compassionate toward others, but at times she was blunt and straight forward, adding an edge to her words and thoughts that forced him to respect her opinion and think of her as an equal.

If this was the manner of women her family raised, then he would admire them as well, for such a person, man or woman, was difficult to find.

* * * *

"How far is it to Summerly?" Jocelyn asked just as the sun was beginning to set on the fourth day of travel.

"Three days more," Tristan answered, propelling her across the camp to the cook's fire where the sweet aroma of roasting meat was wafting through the air.

"Growing weary of traveling, or is it the company that tires you?" he asked, his warm smile never leaving his face.

"Neither, I must say your company has been a welcome distraction. I have endured an array of blundering louts this past year," Jocelyn informed him while she filled her plate with the roasted meat.

Tristan scowled at her for a moment then couldn't help but ask the question silently swirling around in his mind.

"Blundering louts, what use have you for such men?"

"None, I can assure you, though they are certain I have use for them." She followed him back across the camp to the blazing fire in the center and sat down beside him.

"Suitors?" Tristan guessed, assuming he was right by her sudden huff.

"Aye, each and every one come to win Artois, each and every one determined to have what they seek. I have seen men of every kind, age and rank. I will tell you, I am near bound to become a spinster. I need not a man," Jocelyn stated before taking a hardy bite of her dinner.

"Then you must be a wise woman indeed, for I dare say no man would be strong enough to endure you." Tristan laughed loudly when she glared at his words.

He shook his head seeming to know she was far from the sort of woman who would survive the life of a spinster.

"Tell me of these men, I wish to discover if I am acquainted with any of them."

"I believe you might know one. Rhyes…Sir Rhyes. He claimed he fostered with Lord Summerly's son," she supplied, stretching her booted feet out to the fire.

"Aye, I know him, good man," Tristan agreed, nodding his head as he spoke. "Last I heard of him, he was making a name for himself at court. Does he qualify as a blundering lout?" he asked, hardly thinking Rhyes would stoop to such a level.

"In the beginning he did. He was insulting and arrogant. To make him more a fool, he and my captain were endlessly squabbling. But, there seemed to be something more to the man," Jocelyn informed him, seeming to travel to some distant place as she spoke. "I fear he was no lout at all."

"Does he still reside at Artois?" Tristan questioned, pulling her back to herself.

"He was with me the morning you found me," Jocelyn answered, looking at him with sorrowful eyes.

"He was your escort," Tristan stated, beginning to sense that there might have been something growing between his old friend and the lady sitting beside him.

"Aye, though I am certain he would not have perished from his wound. In truth, I know not if he was overrun when he sent me away. He forced me to leave him, thinking I could make it to the keep.

"Rhyes struck my horse when I would not do as he said." She shook her head and sighed deeply.

Jocelyn placed her dinner aside before drawing up her knees, hugging them fiercely.

Tristan allowed the silence to best them both and remained beside her, his eyes fixed on the snapping flames.

She was a remarkable woman; he could see why Rhyes would pursue her. The man needed a holding of his own; Rhyes also needed land and a title for he had none.

What of Jocelyn?

She seemed so much deeper than the sort of woman who would seek for a marriage built on an alliance. What of Lord Milberk, why was he not finding a husband for his daughter?

Tristan pulled his eyes from the fire and smiled at the woman; her head was resting on her drawn up knees, her eyes gently closed against the glow of the flames.

She looked to be nothing more than a traveling urchin. Her cheeks were dirt smudged, her hair falling loose from its braid, but even so, she pulled at a part of his heart he thought would never be awakened.

Tristan shook the soft feeling aside, blaming it on his weariness and laid back on the grass.

If his father were to pass from this madness that plagued him, Tristan would need to think of his sister's future before his own.

To marry off five sisters would be a task that would consume his life for a good many years.

Tristan felt an amused smile creep over his lips with the thought of each and every one of the imps, even as he pitied the men who took them for their wives.

Chapter Eight

"We stop here," Tristan announced when they approached a small bustling village.

They were but two days ride from Summerly. He could tell they were all in need a of much needed rest. He'd been pushing them since they left Artois five days past, he would not push them further.

It was Midsummer's eve and the villagers were preparing the green for the festivities that were to take place that evening.

The rich smell of roasting meat and finely filled pastries were swimming though the air, causing his stomach to growl with the thought of a fine meal rather than whatever could be gathered on the road.

They stopped in the yard of a small inn that was nestled neatly near the center of town. He helped Jocelyn to her feet, gave orders for his men to wait in the yard before escorting her into the small common room of the inn.

It had more of a small cottage-like feel to it rather than the bustling chaos of many of the inns he visited in the past.

"Might I help you?" the innkeeper asked, entering the room from a door in the far wall.

He was no older than Tristan; stout and smiling, seeming to hope they were seeking lodgings.

"Aye, the lady will take your finest room and I will gladly accept anything else you might have to offer," Tristan informed him, not realizing that his hand was lingering on the small of Jocelyn's back.

"Good enough…Beth," the young innkeeper called through the doorway. "My wife, Beth," he informed them when the woman appeared. "Would you be so kind as to take the lady to our best chamber?"

"Aye, come with me." Beth smiled at Jocelyn and beckoned for her to follow as she made for the small staircase.

Tristan watched them go then turned to the innkeeper to pay for their night stay.

"I have seven men traveling with me, good man, might they have use of your stables for the night?" Tristan asked as he paid the man, making sure to offer him extra for the use of his stable.

"Very well. Your room, Sir, is at the top of the stairs only room on the left. I hope you find it to your liking," The innkeeper offered, making to the door to see his other guests to the stables and to no doubt make certain there were only seven as he was told.

"Anything is better than the hard ground, many thanks." Tristan mounted the stairs as the good wife was making her way from the Chamber at the far end of the narrow corridor.

She was nearly the same size as Jocelyn though perhaps a bit broader in the shoulder and slightly shorter.

"Might I help you with something, Sir?" Beth asked, eyeing him skeptically.

"Have you a gown I might purchase for my lady friend?" Tristan boldly asked, causing her to scowl at him.

"I have but one other," Beth answered, ready to push past him.

"Might she borrow it then?" he inquired, causing her to turn and scowl at him yet again.

"Has she none of her own?" Beth hotly questioned.

"Not with her…we left with all haste, all she has is what she is wearing at this time. I vow I will make it worth your while and ensure that it is returned to you in the same manner in which it was borrowed." Tristan placed his hand over his heart as he promised, hoping she would agree.

"Very well," Beth sighed and turned to make her way down the stairs. "Wait where you are I will be but a moment."

In no time at all she returned, bringing with her a vibrant red gown.

"Mind she cares for it well." Beth passed it off to him, receiving a few coins in return for her sacrifice and was on her way.

Tristan smiled at the garment as he made his way through the narrow corridor to knock on Jocelyn's closed door.

She pulled open the structure, took one look at his smiling face and raised her brow at him in question.

"What are you about?" Jocelyn asked, leaning against the doorframe to fold her arms.

She was beginning to know Tristan well enough to know that when he looked mischievous, it was because he was up to something.

"I come bearing borrowed gifts," Tristan informed her as he extended the dress to her.

"Borrowed?" she asked, reaching out to gingerly take the gown from his outstretched arms. "Oh, it is lovely."

"Aye…and borrowed so be kind to it. I thought you might enjoy dressing as a woman for tonight's festivities," he suggested, scowling at her worn tunic.

"Tired of me dressed as a man, are you?" Jocelyn mocked, acting as though she was irritated with his statement.

"I might ask the good innkeeper if he has a spare tunic you might wear if that would suit you better?" he mused, reaching for the gown as he spoke.

"Nay, I like it!"

Jocelyn jumped aside when Tristan tried to take his gift back and laughed when he pursued her across the chamber.

"I come bringing gifts and you snub me, sweet Lady, I am truly hurt." Tristan reached out to snatch the gift from her hands, missing his chance when she hugged the gown to her and sidestepped him.

"I will gladly wear the gown," Jocelyn laughed, trying to keep him at arms-length.

"I only had your comforts in mind," Tristan ranted, sounding truly as though she had no intention of wearing his offering.

"Tristan, I want to wear the gown!" Jocelyn squealed when he caught hold of her about the waist from behind and spun her in a circle.

"Very well," he conceded with a rich laugh. With that Tristan released her and made for the door, calling over his shoulder as he went.

"I will meet you in the yard in an hour. Make haste I am positively famished."

Jocelyn shook her head at him when he closed the door; his footfalls fading down the hallway.

"Fool man," she muttered to herself even as she couldn't help but smile.

She'd been right in assuming he was a man who enjoyed his life. Tristan was content with who he was and his positive attitude and light humor were infectious.

When she was with him, Jocelyn felt more at ease with her life than she had in the last two years.

She was, at one time, a good deal like Tristan, very little troubled her and laughter and jesting were a daily affair.

She placed the gown on the bed and wondered if she had time to bathe before he came looking for her. She quickly decided she deserved a bath. She'd been traveling for five days with nothing other than the clothes on her back.

He could wait a while longer.

Tristan paced the yard wondering what could be keeping her. Perhaps the gown didn't fit; mayhap she'd fallen asleep?

He folded his arms and looked in the direction of the village green. He could hear the sounds of music and revelry, as well as smell the luscious scent of the fare drifting to his nose on the gentle breeze.

Tristan turned back to the inn, ready to go in search of her only to find a woman dressed in a striking red gown standing in the doorway.

Her rich auburn hair was no longer braided but flowing down the length of her back, her features were no longer drawn. She seemed refreshed and relaxed as she stared at him, her eyes full of amusement.

"Lady Artois is it you?" Tristan questioned, squinting at her when she approached.

"Sir Tristan?" Jocelyn asked in return.

"It is remarkable," he mused when she came to a stop before him.

"What?" she asked, squinting up at him as though she knew not what he saw different in her.

"I once thought you to be a man." Tristan laughed when she struck him on the arm; her pale green eyes alight with amusement.

"Come with me, Lady. I thought I might waste away waiting for you."

"It is good for a man to wait for a woman," Jocelyn assured him, accepting his offered arm.

"Waiting is the job of a husband, I beg you to save your tarrying for him," Tristan jested. "Awe, blessed food!" he announced when they reached the green and he could, at long last, quiet his snarling innards.

They ate their fill and sat looking on until the sun sunk from the sky and the music grew louder, bringing the young and old alike to their work-worn feet to dance about the blazing fires.

Jocelyn took no time in joining in the festivities; she left Tristan where he sat on the grass to dance freely about the nearest fire.

He watched her from afar as she joined hands with the other young women, spinning and laughing as though she was an enchanted forest sprite.

Tristan couldn't help but smile at the sight of her. All her worries were truly cast aside, showing him for the first time the radiant woman she was in truth.

Tristan pushed to his feet and crossed the distance to where she danced, eager to join the joyful woman before her seemingly boundless energy expired.

Jocelyn danced and laughed, her heart lightened along with her feet as she spun about to the merry music.

Oh how long it had been since she was allowed to feel this kind of freedom.

She felt her feet unwillingly stop their movement with that thought as she recalled the last time she'd taken part in the Midsummer's eve festivities.

It was before she'd come to Artois, and only months before Bart was killed.

Her eyes came into focus on Tristan as he walked toward her, a wide smile fixed to his mouth, his hair seemed lighter in the night, causing her memories to rush over her in a flood so consuming she nearly fell to her knees.

Bart had been there that night; he was visiting her uncle at Norick, joining in the revelry as she was. Bart was there for Meredith, but it mattered little to Jocelyn if he was there for another woman, for she knew her cousin hardly thought of him as anything more than a brother.

Meredith was blind to his affection toward her as Bart was to the affection Jocelyn held for him.

Jocelyn danced with him that night. She'd imagined then that it was she Bart cared for, that he looked upon her with all the devotion and longing he showed to her dear cousin.

Bart had held her hands in his for the length of a single dance, causing her pulse to quicken and her flesh to warm with his touch.

"Jocelyn…Jocelyn?" Tristan's concerned voice pulled her from her trance, bringing her to the realization that he was gripping her hands in his, his eyes searching her face with worry.

"Are you unwell?" Tristan asked as she shook off her daydreaming and looked at him in truth.

"Aye," Jocelyn answered, taking a mighty breath into her lungs.

"You looked as though you were miles away," Tristan stated, pulling her from midst of the dancers to a quiet corner of the yard.

"I thought for a moment that you were someone else," Jocelyn answered, wishing she had better control over her wandering mind.

"Who?" Tristan inquired, following after her when she made her way back into the swirling crowd.

"It matters not," Jocelyn answered, "he is dead and I am in desperate need of a new memory of this night."

She turned when they reached the frolicking couples, ignored the questions in his eyes and took hold of his hands, determined to push the memory of Bart from her mind.

Even if it was for one night, she wanted to be fully free of her sorrow.

"Jocelyn, you are crying," Tristan informed her, before she could entice him to dance.

Tristan reached out and tenderly smoothed a tear from her cheek. Jocelyn followed his hand with her own, scowling at the tears she wiped from her face.

"Aye," she whispered, biting her lip for a moment in frustration.

"Why must it be so difficult to let go?" she muttered, refusing to look at Tristan even when he took hold of her chin in his hand and tipped her face up.

"Do you wish to return to the inn?" Tristan asked, his voice so low she could barely hear it over the ruckus around them.

"Aye," Jocelyn quietly answered, her determination was lost for the moment. There was no use struggling to make new memories when the old refused to be forgotten.

Just before midday Tristan led the small group of travelers through the gates of Summerly. The welcoming smell of the sea rolled through the air, greeting them with its salty aroma.

The keep was more an ominous fortress than Jocelyn expected it to be. The bulk of it butted up against the cliff's edge, its mighty wall towering around the remainder of the castle, protecting it against any who would claim to be an enemy.

For the remaining day's journey, they never discussed what took place on Midsummers eve. Tristan had the feeling her comment about letting go had everything to do with the woman she'd become.

He'd seen her merrily dancing one moment then weeping and melancholy the next. He also saw the way she looked at him when he took hold of her hands, ready to lead her in a dance. Jocelyn had been looking into the face of someone she cherished. He'd seen it in her eyes and felt it in the way she took hold of his hands, she was holding on to something that was at one time taken from her.

Tristan had not the heart to ask her who the man was. He could only feel that the loss of this man had everything to do with why she had not yet taken it upon herself to marry.

He hoped there would come a time when she would trust him enough to confide in him, to share that difficult time in her past. Until then, he would let it be.

The shouts of his sisters met his ears well before they came to a stop in the yard.

Their raised voices pulled him from his silent thoughts to the door of the keep.

The group of girls were bounding down the stairs, their voices filled with excitement as though they were truly happy to see him returned.

"Prepare yourself, sweet Lady, for I fear they will smother you in their excitement," Tristan warned, his heart warming slightly with her amused laugh.

"Saints preserve us all!" Tristan bellowed to the swarm of young women.

He dismounted and entered the mass of girls, hugging each in turn as he chastised them for acting like wild beasts rather than well-bred young ladies.

"I shall put you all out to pasture, or I will surely go deaf from your shrillness," Tristan teased.

"Did you bring her?" Bethany asked, clinging to his arm.

"Who?" he questioned, seeming not to know what she was talking about.

"Our aunt told us you were bringing back a grand lady," Mary informed him, her pale green eyes alight with excitement. "Where is she?"

"Hush the lot of you," Mona chided from where she was quickly descending the stairs.

"Did you not bring her?" Bethany ranted, clearly disappointed in her brother.

"I brought her, leave me be vultures and I will present her to you." Tristan pushed free of the mass of them and made his way to where Jocelyn was looking down in amusement from the safety of her mount.

"You must fend for yourself," Tristan warned, "I am but one man."

He placed Jocelyn on her feet and turned, managing to speak before his sisters could erupt in a rush of questions.

"Might I present, Lady Jocelyn of Artois. Jocelyn, my sisters. Bethany who is the eldest, Mary, Millie, Anne and poor Norissa who is but eight summers and is forced to be the youngest."

"I am pleased to meet you all. Your brother has so many good things to say about you." Jocelyn greeted, smiling brightly at Norissa when she stepped forward to get a better look at their guest.

"Know you you're dressed like a man?" Norissa asked, placing her hands on her hips.

"So I have been told," Jocelyn answered, only to be swarmed by a throng of questions from the other girls.

"Do you always dress as a man?"

"I thought a grand lady would be dressed in fine satin."

"Do you own fine gowns?"

"Look Millie, she is wearing a sword…is my brother and his men not enough to protect you?"

"Enough, the lot of you," Tristan defended, coming to stand between the lady and his sisters. "Away, and allow her to breathe. You may pester her with your questions later."

Jocelyn watched the lot of them scurry up the stairs laughing and chattering wildly as they went.

"I have struggled to teach them better manners, but I am at a loss. This is my poor aunt, Mona, Lord Summerly's sister," Tristan offered, gesturing to his aunt.

Jocelyn nodded to the woman, noting she looked drained. Her eyes were the same pale green as Tristan's and his sisters, her once dark hair graying and struggling to remain restrained by the crisp wimple she wore.

"Where is my father?" Tristan asked, leading them up the stairs and into the hall.

"Confined, he has been asking for you since you left." Mona longed to tell him that her father sent for Doyle, but feared she couldn't in front of their guest.

Tristan quietly nodded then turned to Jocelyn, smiling at her warmly through his worry.

"Go with my aunt, she will show you your chamber and see that you have everything you need to make you comfortable. I will visit my father and tell him you are here. I will see you again this evening," he promised.

"Are you certain? I can go with you now," Jocelyn assured, knowing she probably looked horrid, but she was eager to visit with Lord Summerly.

"Rest, you may see him this evening." Tristan briefly took hold of her hand before disappearing up the far stairwell.

Chapter Nine

Day drifted into early evening and then to night and still Jocelyn had seen nothing of Tristan. In her worry, she set out on her own to find him and make certain all was well with his father.

He told her he would see her that evening, but he wasn't at dinner, giving her cause to believe his father was worse off than he originally thought.

She'd passed the last handful of hours in the lady's solar with his aunt and sisters, but she was beginning to worry when it was time for the young women to retire and there was still no word from him.

"Tristan?" Jocelyn called out from the entry of the great hall.

Jocelyn could clearly see him sitting in a chair beside the hearth, but still he never answered her.

She lifted the hem of her borrowed lavender gown and quietly came to stand beside him.

"Tristan?" she questioned when still he didn't acknowledge her.

"He is not himself," Tristan whispered, his voice filled with a kind of anger she'd never heard him express.

"What mean you?" Jocelyn asked, resting a hand on his shoulder.

"He remembers nothing of the Lady of Artois, he knows not who you are and so I have brought you all this way for nothing." Tristan reached up and took hold of the hand she'd placed on his shoulder and held it for a moment before leaning forward to rest his head in his hands.

"Forgive me, I should have known better than to drag you all this way at the request of a madman. I knew he was not himself when I left and yet I fulfilled his bidding."

"There is nothing to forgive," Jocelyn assured, walking around his chair, kneeling down before him, giving him no choice but to look at her.

"I would very much like to see him," Jocelyn requested, looking deeply into his eyes to make certain he knew she meant what she was saying.

Tristan looked at her for a moment, his brows drawn into a scowl.

"My aunt and sisters got their hands on you," Tristan stated, looking her over in the glowing light of the fire.

Her hair was neatly braided and wrapped into a knot at the base of her neck; her men's clothes were replaced with a fine lavender gown that was pooled about her as she knelt before him.

"Aye, your sisters informed me that it was not fit for a lady, such as myself, to dress like a man. I believe this was once your aunt's gown, before she came to look after your sisters," she explained.

"It suits you," he remarked, sounding a bit too serious.

"Come…take me to see your father. Perhaps once he sees me, he will remember who I am and why he sent you to fetch me." She took hold of his hands and pulled him to his feet, giving him little choice but to obey.

Tristan kept her hand in his and led her up the stairwell to the lord's private chamber.

Jocelyn could feel his apprehension when Tristan opened the door and pulled her across the room to the large curtained bed where his father rested, propped up against a mound of pillows.

Mortan looked terribly pale and frail to Jocelyn's eyes, much more so than when he left Artois.

"Father?" Tristan asked, gaining the man's attention.

Mortan opened his eyes and looked at his son, though for a moment, Jocelyn wondered if he truly saw him for his eyes were hollow and glazed over, seeming to see nothing at all.

"I have brought Lady Artois to you as you asked," Tristan informed him.

"Artois?" Mortan mumbled, looking to the woman at his son's side. "I know not this place, but you are most welcome here. To where is it you are traveling?" he asked, squinting his eyes as he looked her over.

"I have come to see you, my Lord," Jocelyn offered, smiling at him warmly.

"Did you come here on your own? Where is your escort?" Mortan inquired, looking about the room for the man in question.

"I traveled with your son. Tristan brought me here to Summerly." She glanced at Tristan, gently squeezing his hand when she beheld the hurt in his eyes.

"Are you betrothed to my son?" Mortan questioned, turning the pallor of her skin crimson.

"Nay father," Tristan answered, releasing her to place his hand on the small of her back as he spoke to the delirious man. "She is a dear friend; she only wished to see you."

"Awe, I see," Mortan remarked, though it was clear to both of them that he was still confused.

"It was a pleasure to meet you, my Lord." Jocelyn gave him a slight bow and turned Tristan from the chamber, hoping she might be able to help him through this challenge.

"I am sorry, Tristan," Jocelyn offered when they were once again in the corridor, the chamber door firmly closed behind them.

"This is not of your doing. I should have seen it coming. He has not been himself for months, why even before my father left for Artois he was not the man I remember him to be." Tristan turned them back down the corridor to the stairwell.

"Left *for* Artois?" Jocelyn questioned when they reached the great hall and made for the hearth, for it was the only place in the mighty room that was lit against the night.

"Your father told me he was journeying home. I clearly remember him telling me he wintered with family near the border."

Tristan sat down across from her and shook his head with her words.

"Nay, we have no kin near the border. He left here intent on traveling to Artois. When I insisted that I make the journey with him, he became angry and ordered me to look after my aunt and sisters."

Jocelyn allowed his words to mull about in her mind for a moment, struggling to push aside the nagging inkling that Lord Summerly might have been after what all the others were seeking when they entered the walls of her home.

Alas, he did not seem like the others, he never once spoke to her of marriage. He seemed to her as nothing more than what he claimed to be.

"Why would he lie to me?" Jocelyn asked after a moment of quiet reflection.

"I know not. This is a puzzle to me as well. He was not always as you see him now. My father was a grand man, honorable and witty. He was the sort of man a friend or relation could count on in a time of need. Of late, he is merely a shell of who he once was."

"What will you do now, Tristan?" Jocelyn asked, reaching out to take hold of his hand, wanting nothing more than to help him through this challenge.

"I will take over in my father's place, there seems to be nothing more that can be done," he answered, rubbing his thumb over her fingers as he spoke.

It was as though they'd known one another for the whole of their lives.

Jocelyn felt safe in his company, at ease and comforted as she would with Tomas or her father. She could only assume Tristan felt the same.

"I would help you in whatever way I can," Jocelyn assured. "I know a good deal about the workings of a holding such as this, I might help with the household or sort out the ledgers with you," she offered.

"Is there nothing you cannot accomplish?" Tristan asked, his mouth turning up in a smile.

"Plenty," she guaranteed while in her mind she was going through every wrong she longed to right in her own life.

"It is the same as before," Jocelyn remarked, rubbing her temples as she spoke.

Her eyes were weary from studying the many documents and books scattered across the desk before her.

Tristan had thought there was a mistake and asked her to look over them and so she had, twice, and still she came up with the same daunting conclusion.

Summerly was in a dire state.

"Aye," Tristan muttered, sitting back in his chair with a disconcerted huff. "Why would he not tell me of this?"

"Pride perhaps. I hardly think it would be easy to tell an heir that there is nothing left for them but debt. Surely he must have known better than to let it go this far," Jocelyn mused.

"Why was he not taking better care of his holdings? Summerly's lands are vast and at one time they produced more than enough income to support a keep of this size." She flipped through a few of the ledgers before her, her brow furrowing with the carelessness written out by Mortan's own hand.

"Think you it might be mended?" Tristan asked, standing to walk around the desk to look over her shoulder.

"I strive to believe anything is possible, though I know not if there is time to mend it before those to whom he is indebted come breaking down upon you demanding what they are owed."

"What of the tenants?" Tristan inquired, his breath falling against the back of her neck as he leaned further over to gesture at the writing before them.

Jocelyn cleared her throat with his closeness, slightly bewildered with the strange feeling that caused her heart to flutter.

"You could raise the rents and call in their debts, but there still would not be enough to make a dramatic difference and you run the risk of making the situation worse. If those who serve you are not able to live, then your livelihood will suffer as well." Jocelyn felt him nod; all the while attempting to keep her breathing even for fear he would sense the sudden rush of her pulse.

"Then what think you? What would you do if it was Artois that was suffering?" Tristan questioned, causing her to turn and look up at him.

"I would never let such a thing happen to Artois," she stated with solid conviction, poking him in the chest with her finger.

"You must see to your holdings, call in those who run your lands. You might need to have a tighter reign over them for the time being. We must discover why that which was once prosperous is not any longer."

"What about those whom my father owes?" Tristan asked, the entirety of all she was telling him weighing heavily on his heart.

"Meet with them as well, perhaps they will grant you leniency when they know what has become of your father and discover that you are struggling to make it right." Jocelyn turned her face from him and absently tapped her finger on the desk, not knowing what else to say or do with his silence.

"How did you become so wise?" Tristan questioned, smiling at her for a moment before pushing back and returning to the opposite side of the desk to begin the task of sorting through the stack of parchment.

"I am a woman," Jocelyn teased, "truly it is nothing at all to be wise."

"Indeed," Tristan laughed, shaking his head at her while he continued to sort through the documents.

Jocelyn pushed to her feet and made her way quietly from his father's study, leaving Tristan for a moment to carry on without her.

She was in need of a distraction and feared what she sought wouldn't be found confined to the study.

Tristan lifted a ledger that rested on Jocelyn's side of the desk and found himself frowning at the careful writing upon it.

The contract was recent, dated only a month past. It carried his father's signature as well as one that caused the flesh on his arms to bristle.

Doyle, his father vowed years ago to never employ the man again. He'd given them all his word, but this single document belied every ounce of trust Tristan once held for his father.

There was nothing stating what it was his father had employed the man to do, it only held their signatures as well as the sum that was owed upon the completion of the task.

Tristan folded the bit of parchment and tucked it into the pocket of his surcoat before making his way to the lady's solar.

He knew his father would entrust no one in his plotting, but still, he wanted to know if his aunt knew anything of this.

Moments later he stood in the doorway of the solar, looking into the room as though he was invisible, relishing the tender scene before him.

Jocelyn sat on the cushioned seat of the alcove, her knees drawn up to allow her arms to wrap about them. His sisters were scattered about her, enjoying the conversation as well as the merry bit of sunlight spilling through the open window.

"Artois is a good way from here, I am not blessed with the view of the sea, but the forest surrounding the keep is vast and beautiful," Jocelyn remarked, clearly in answer to one of their questions.

"I believe I would miss the sea," Bethany mused where she sat on the floor, her mending scattered about her lap. "Do you miss Artois?"

"Aye…but I will return soon enough." Jocelyn glanced to the doorway, smiling at Tristan for a moment before another question was thrown her way.

Tristan returned the smile and struggled to ignore the strange feeling the sight of her stirred within him.

He was comfortable in her company more so than any woman he'd ever known. She was bright and full of spirit. When she allowed herself to let go of the sorrow she was holding deep within her soul, she radiated with a blinding infectious light. She was a joy and Tristan felt blessed to have her in his life during this trying time.

Tristan pulled his eyes from the group of young women to where his aunt was silently mending a gown in the corner of the room. Mona seemed to sense his eyes upon her for she stood, placed her mending on the chair, crossed to where he stood and followed her nephew into the corridor.

"Is something the matter?" Mona asked when he remained silent for a long while.

"I have been looking over the ledgers and found something that disturbed me," Tristan answered.

He stopped their walking midway down the corridor to face her.

Mona brushed back a strand of graying hair that always managed to escape the confines of her wimple and nodded.

"Doyle," Mona stated, shocking him slightly.

"Aye, know you why my father sent for him?" Tristan asked, searching her face as he spoke.

Mona was once a bright young woman. Tristan remembered vividly the day his aunt came to live at Summerly. She was so far from the drawn and worried being she was now; the stress of seeing to the responsibility of raising her brother's daughters had clearly worn on her. Mona had never been given the opportunity to seek out a life of her own and now as he looked into her faded eyes he felt slightly guilty for the hardships placed on her shoulders by his father.

"Nay, my brother ordered me to send for him. I knew he was not himself, but I feared for what he might do if I refused.

"Your father remembers not that Doyle was summoned, but I fear the horrid man will return seeking his payment. The foul man will not be made to leave without it." Mona began wringing her hands, looking at Tristan for the reassurance she so desperately needed.

Doyle frightened her beyond all reason, the man possessed an evil she could clearly feel, but was unable to explain.

Mona was certain little good would come from him returning to Summerly.

"There is no need to fear," Tristan assured, reaching out to place a hand on her shoulder. "I will mend this."

"How…there is so much your father has neglected these last years?" she whispered, for fear someone might hear their conversation.

"I will start with the tenants as well as my father's creditors. I can do nothing more." Tristan was at a loss, there was nothing more he could do but begin to right the wrongs of his father. If he was to come out the victor, he knew he would have to make haste.

If Summerly failed, there would be no hope left for his sisters. Without a strong holding behind them, he would never supply his kinswomen with husbands. His father should have known better than this.

How could he neglect his family obligations so fully?

Tristan offered his aunt a small smile, hoping she was reassured for the moment and made his way down the corridor to the lord's chamber.

There was no time like the present to begin righting the past. First, he would pay a visit to his father and see if by some stroke of luck the man remembered something, anything, of the last month.

If his father could recall nothing, he would have no choice but to deal with Doyle when he reappeared and hope that whatever the man was employed to do was not of a vile nature.

He knew what Doyle was capable of. He'd seen the man's handy work years ago. If the price was right, the man would have no reserve in selling his soul to the very devil. Doyle possessed no honor and even less respect for life.

His very existence revolved around wealth and if a person was willing to pay a hefty sum to employ the horrid man, then Doyle cared not the task, as long as he was working for the highest bidder.

Tristan knocked lightly on his father's door then let himself into the dreary chamber.

Mortan was sleeping, propped up against his pillows. His eyes closed against the little light that was allowed in through the closed shutters.

He looked no better than he had the previous day. Tristan's stomach tied into a thick knot when he crossed the chamber to look down on the man who was once larger than life.

Mortan was once a good man. There was a time he was Tristan's hero, a man who could do no wrong. But now, all Tristan saw before was a hollow shell of the man he once was.

Now it was left to his son to sort out his past wrongs and mend them before it was too late.

Chapter Ten

Robin stood on the battlements, looking to the small party of men approaching the keep. They rode under the white flag, hoping to gain entrance to the fortress.

A fortnight they'd been held within the keep. A fortnight with no word of his daughter or a reason as to why Artois was being held under siege.

Supplies were running slim, if they were not released from this torment soon, those residing within the walls of Artois would suffer greatly.

Robin felt the apprehension of the two men who stood by his side and feared they suffered greater than he. Not only for Jocelyn's disappearance, but also for the punishment he himself ordered upon them.

Rhyes and Tomas seemed bent on quarreling over whom was at fault for their present state, as well as any other menial thing that happened to cross their path.

On the second day, Robin had stomached all he could bear of their constant fighting and came to the conclusion that he either lock them both away in the dungeon or force them to be civil.

So, after a moment of reflection, Robin did what he would have done to any of his children if they acted in such a childish way.

Robin commanded they pass every moment, of every day, in one another's company. Tomas and Rhyes stood watch together, passed their time in the lists together, ate meals and slept as though they were the closest of brothers.

After the first three hours of their punishment, Robin was certain he would be burying both of them before the sunset, but by noon, the following day, they seemed to have nothing more to say to one another, other than what was absolutely necessary to survive.

"To the yard," Robin ordered when the gates were open to their enemy. "It is time we discover what it is they're after."

Moments later the trio stood before a menacing black haired man and the five minions he brought with him. His eyes were deep and calculating, seeming to miss nothing as he stood before them.

Rhyes took the place on Robin's left and Tomas on his right, each radiating a deep anger Robin feared might snap at any moment.

"Will you not invite us in?" Doyle boldly asked, his mouth stretched into a sneer. "Or is the only hospitality we will be offered the dust of the yard."

"The yard will serve you well enough," Robin informed him, his stomach clenched as he beheld the sinister man. "I would know your business here."

"A simple errand to be sure. How fares the Lady of Artois?" Doyle questioned, seeming to enjoy the effect his words had on the men before him.

Doyle produced the ring he'd been given, when they made no comment he held it out so they all might see it.

"She is missing, is she not?" Doyle asked, biting further at Robin's stretched nerves.

"Where is she?" Tomas hissed, his hand gripping the hilt of his sword.

"Missing," Doyle stated, in answer to the question, his sneer growing in size. "I myself would have no qualms in returning her…for a fee."

"Mercenaries," Rhyes murmured, shifting his feet in the dirt.

They all should have guessed as much.

Doyle began to laugh at the comment, his irksome voice cutting into Rhyes resolve until Rhyes was convinced the man had taken Jocelyn hostage and even now, as the fiend stood laughing at his enemy, she could be suffering.

"Very good," Doyle smirked. "What say you Lord Milberk? What would you give to have your daughter back?" Doyle inquired, tossing the ring to Robin who caught it neatly in his outstretched hand.

"What is it you seek?" Robin asked, fearing he already knew the answer.

"Wealth, my Lord. Artois is a wealthy keep, is it not?" Doyle held his hands out gesturing to the massive stone fortress behind them. "I would have Artois."

"Artois is not mine to give," Robin informed him, reaching out to place a hand on Rhyes shoulder when he took a step forward.

The rules of combat forbid them to attack their enemy as long as they entered the holdings under the white flag. Robin was a man of honor; such rules bound him to where he stood even though he felt like lunging forward himself.

"Then you will not see the face of your daughter. Relinquish Artois and I will tell you where your daughter is. Refuse and you will never see her again," Doyle threatened.

Robin could tell from the look in his sinister eyes that he would hold true to his threat.

Rhyes could bear this man no longer; Doyle's threat attacked his own pride, for he knew it was his fault Jocelyn had been taken.

He pulled free of Robin's hold and flew forward, tackling the stunned mercenary, sending them both sprawling to the dust.

Rhyes retrieved his knife from his belt and held it to Doyle's neck to pin the man to the ground before any could move.

"You go against the rules of combat," Doyle breathed, holding remarkably still under the pressure of Rhyes' knife.

"As far as I am concerned, the rules do not apply to ruffians such as yourself! Discard your weapons or your leader will be no more!" Rhyes shouted to the stunned mercenaries who obliged his order with little hesitation.

"Now we might negotiate in truth," Rhyes informed him, maintaining his dominating position. "Whom do you serve?" he asked, his voice low and threatening.

"You waste your time," Doyle wheezed, the edge of the knife pressing into his flesh, causing him to instantly regret his comment.

Robin and Tomas stood back watching as their enemy started to look less menacing and more as a man who was near panic.

"You work for the highest bidder, do you not? Tell me man, what value do you place on your own life? I for one value it very little and will pry the information I need from your men while you rot." Rhyes pushed down on the knife as he spoke, his anger and need for vengeance blinding him momentarily.

"Tell me!" he demanded.

"Summerly…Lord Mortan of Summerly," Doyle supplied, his eyes tightly closed against the menacing face of the man who hovered above him.

"Summerly? What use is she to Lord Summerly?" Rhyes asked, pulling back slightly so the man might have an easier time speaking.

"I did not care to ask, the old fool is destitute. I have a mind to think that after he pays me that which I'm owed, there will be nothing left to him. Perhaps, he will use the wench for ransom himself."

Rhyes punched Doyle full across the face with his insulting remark, refusing to listen to him talk about Jocelyn in such a way.

"You will watch your tongue when speaking of the lady." Rhyes took Doyle by the front of his mailed shirt and hefted him to his feet, looking him square in the eye as he spoke, making certain he heard each and every word.

"I am now the highest bidder. You will ride with us to Summerly and you will help my men, as well as Lord Milberk's in seeing Lady Artois safely returned to her kin. Only when the lady is free will I consider allowing you to live. Betray me and it will be the end of your miserable life." Rhyes shook him as he spoke, making certain every single word was pounded into his thick skull.

Tomas listened intently to the exchange from where he stood beside Robin. Both their swords were drawn, their eyes intently fixed on the five other men Doyle brought with him.

Tomas had never seen a man as threatening as Rhyes was at that moment. He had a feeling the mercenary was thinking the same, for the pallor of his skin had turned sickly.

Tomas watched the fiend nod in agreement to Rhyes threat and only then was Doyle released to stand freely before the man he now served.

"Gather your men," Rhyes ordered, "I will waste no more time within these walls."

Doyle nodded and made his way from the yard, clearly fuming as he went.

"How can you trust him?" Tomas asked once he was out of hearing.

"The man values his life," Rhyes answered, returning his knife to its sheath. "Even as he knows I do not. Are you ready my Lord?" he asked, turning his attention to Robin.

"Aye," Robin answered, still slightly shocked with what had just taken place.

"Tell me Rhyes…do you value your life?" Robin asked, the gravity of his question cutting though the thickness in the air.

"Nay…not when I have wronged such a lady as your daughter, my Lord. I vow to you that I will return Jocelyn to her home at the cost of my very life." Rhyes gave Robin a respectful bow before pushing past him to bellow for his men.

"Think you he is mad?" Robin asked, looking to Tomas.

"Aye," Tomas answered, truly humbled to admit that Rhyes had just gained a bit of his respect.

Chapter Eleven

Tristan looked to the woman riding beside him and found himself scowling with the frustrated expression on her lovely face.

They'd spent the day in the village speaking with a number of his tenants, as well as the overseers, informing them of the changes that were to take place.

Jocelyn was right in assuming that things were not as they once were.

It seemed some of his tenants had prospered greatly at the expense of their Lord.

They found near a dozen men and a handful of women who had gone about pocketing the earnings that should have gone to the keep.

There were other offences as well. The fields belonging to the keep were not being tended as carefully as they ought to be.

Tristan offered a mighty threat to those who were to blame for this lack in discipline. There would be no punishment as of now, but if matters did not improve, the dungeons of Summerly would be filled with those who refused to abide by the law.

The fields had been sewn as they were every year in the past; they would see a grand harvest in the fall if they were prudently tended. He would be a fool if he stood by as his father did in the past and let the fruits of his lands pass through his fingers.

Tristan was determined to set right his father's slackened rule and restore Summerly's good name, not only for himself, but for his sisters. They were innocent in this; they would have a bleak future if he failed them.

"You look drained," Tristan commented, pulling her attention from her own thoughts and to the man riding beside her.

They'd spent the last two days confined to the study, painstakingly writing to those Summerly owed, explaining the situation and ensuring he would see the debts fully repaid in all haste.

Today was no better, they were outdoors, but disciplining ones tenants hardly made for an enjoyable time.

It was a tedious handful of days, but for Tristan, they seemed to be made a bit easier because of the woman working diligently by his side.

"As do you," Jocelyn answered. "Your thoughts should be on the pressing problems surrounding you, not on me."

"I have grown tired of problems for the whole of one day," Tristan sighed, looking behind them to the crisp blue sky rising above the line of roughly built houses.

"Come with me."

He turned his mount back the way they came and led them through the narrow lanes until they broke free of the village and surrounding fields, finally entering the wild meadowlands that lined the jagged cliffs.

"Where are you going?" Jocelyn called from behind him, urging her mount to keep up with his haste.

Moments later she pulled the animal to a stop beside his and looked out over the rolling sea.

"It is beautiful," Jocelyn observed, her words edged with a sigh.

"Aye, my father and I use to ride along these cliffs when I was a lad, I have not been out this far since I went away to foster." Tristan dismounted and stood looking out over the rolling water below.

As a young man, he enjoyed the freedom of looking out over the sea. Many a time in his youth he would stand on the edge of the cliffs and feel as though he was a bird in flight with nothing hindering his movements, nothing holding him back from the joy he longed for.

"Is it not sad how we put aside the happiness of our youth for the everyday sorrows of adulthood," Jocelyn commented, coming to stand beside him.

"Sorrows?" Tristan questioned, looking at her in bewilderment.

"Do you never long for your childhood?" she asked, her voice turning wistful.

"Nay, I relish the memory of it, but never do I long to relive it. Do you?" Tristan asked, studying her freely as she continued to look out over the water.

"Aye, life was simple then. There were no decisions to be made, no knowledge of the hardships the world holds; there was only innocent bliss. I would be free of the chains I bear," Jocelyn confessed, feeling the need to step away from the pressing sorrow she felt in her soul.

Her eyes were filled with a longing he'd seen glimpses of in the past, a longing so deep it consumed her and filled her with a sadness he couldn't explain.

"Do you speak of your obligation to Artois?" Tristan asked, longing to know what it was that bound her to sadness.

"Nay, Artois is my home," she answered softly. "Though, I would gladly give it up were it not a part of me. I would be free," she whispered, her eyes closing as she spoke.

"This is where I came in my youth to feel the freedom you speak of. The freedom of the sea and that of the birds who make the cliffs their home." Tristan reached out and took her by the hand. "Come with me," he instructed.

Tristan pulled her in up the cliff line to a grouping of rocks that jutted out over the edge, offering a perilous, but captivating, view of the frothing water below.

Tristan removed his cloak from his shoulders and looked to her confused face with a smile.

As she could not right the struggles he was facing now, he could not right the wrongs of her past, but he could give her freedom.

For but a short moment of her life, he could grant her that which she was seeking.

"What are you about?" Jocelyn asked, her brows drawn together in a familiar scowl.

"I would give you freedom."

Tristan turned her toward the cliff's edge, twisted his cloak into a makeshift sling and placed it about her waist. He gripped the cloak at both ends and gave her a wide smile.

"Walk out to the edge," Tristan instructed, urging her forward.

"I will not!" Jocelyn gasped, ready to free herself of his cloak and make her way back to the safety of the meadow.

"Do you not trust me?" Tristan questioned, holding her captive.

"I know not," Jocelyn answered, struggling to push past him. "I know I have no desire to discover my trust on the edge of a cliff."

"Come…I will let no harm come to you." Tristan turned her back to face the sea; the crisp breeze tugging at them as she quietly struggled with her apprehension.

"And what becomes of me if your hands betray you and release their grip?" she asked heavily.

"I will leap over the edge and follow you to the depths of the sea," Tristan solemnly vowed.

"Comforting," Jocelyn mumbled, clearly far from convinced that standing on a cliff's edge would do anything other than terrify her.

"Trust me, sweet Lady, you should know me well enough by now to know that I would never let harm come to you."

"It has been years since I have so fully trusted a man who is not my kin," Jocelyn stated, her eyes still fixed on the vast view before them.

"I will not betray you," Tristan informed her with serious conviction.

She nodded with his words, took a mighty breath and stepped forward to the cliff's edge.

Jocelyn felt her heart pound so rapidly within her chest she feared it would burst. The breeze pulled and tugged at her hair and gown as her eyes beheld the frothing water beating against the jagged rocks of the shoreline below.

She could feel Tristan tightly gripping the makeshift sling, holding her back from certain death as he swore he would.

In a matter of seconds, her heart eased its rapid thumping as her soul slowly began to absorb the beauty of her precarious perch.

She leaned further out over the edge, her soul lifting slightly as the crisp breeze beat against her and every sorrow that tore at her heart was lifted. She was beginning to feel that as she allowed herself to fully trust the man who held her safe from certain death a part of her heart, that was once closed, was opened once more.

The waves crashed beneath her, the gulls screeched as they glided on the rolling wind. She stretched her arms out as though she was ready to join them, freeing her mind of the past and every concern of her future.

For this one moment, her caged soul felt a sense of true freedom.

Jocelyn held no fear, no hesitation or doubt. Her mind was free of thoughts of loss and sorrow as she felt as though she was soaring with the gulls.

Slowly she came back to herself and allowed Tristan to pull her back to reality.

He took his cloak from about her waist, clasped it around his neck then stood beside her, looking out over the vast stretch of sea.

They stood in tranquil silence, needing to say nothing until the sun began to dip down behind the watery horizon.

"You will miss out on the joys of the now if you continue to dwell on how your past wronged you," Tristan stated, seemingly content where he stood watching the sunset.

"How does one forget?" Jocelyn asked, praying he held the answer.

"Why forget, sweet Lady. What purpose would we have to live and learn if we were to forget? Whatever wrongs committed against you, let them pass, allow your soul to remember how to live."

"I lived for him, I would have thrown my heart at his feet had he asked it of me," she rambled.

Tristan had not asked for such information, but somehow Jocelyn longed for him to know.

"A man," he sighed, her comment confirming what he'd been assuming all along. "You loved him?"

"Aye."

"What became of this man you loved?" Tristan asked, looking on, as the sea seemed to catch fire beneath the rays of the evening sun.

"He died, the same night as my young sister. He fought alongside my kin to free Milberk of the siege that was strangling them." Jocelyn forced her eyes to remain open; for fear that if they closed she would again see Bart's face and feel the despair of losing that which she'd only just gained.

"I am sorry. It is difficult to lose one whom you cherish. You must cling to your happiness, to all the times he held you in his arms and—"

Tristan's words fell still when she turned and looked up at him a slight scowl marring her face as a deep sigh escaped her lips.

"What is it?"

"He did not love me," Jocelyn stated, her heart recognizing her words as truth.

"He never held me in his arms nor did he speak of the life we might share together. He would have wed my cousin had she not loved another." Jocelyn felt a wayward tear roll down her cheek with the solemn confession, but made no attempt to hinder its progress.

"He knew not of my affection for him, not until he lay dying in my arms. I would have lived for him, but I would have loved him in vain. I do not want to be a second to any woman," Jocelyn stated, searching Tristan's face as she spoke.

Jocelyn suddenly laughed with that one single comment and the honesty held within it.

Never before had she felt such conviction. Had Bart lived, had he wed her, would he have ever been thinking of another?

She slowly began to realize what her heart had been longing to tell her.

She would have wasted her life away longing for a love that would never have been and perhaps missed out on a life that might truly bring her happiness.

Bart might have wed her had he lived, but in the back of her mind, Jocelyn would have always wondered if he was thinking of her or her cousin. Would she have ever been enough for a man who loved another?

Tristan reached out his hand and cupped her face, tenderly smoothing away her tear with the pad of his thumb.

"It would seem you have found a piece of yourself that was missing." Tristan remarked, unable to resist granting her an understanding smile.

"Aye." Her cheek seemed to burn beneath his touch, as her heart quickened in a way it never had before.

She'd only known him for a short while, but even so, he was becoming a part of her.

Jocelyn knew his smile, the familiar comfort of his hand on the small of her back and could judge his mood by the tone of his voice.

She looked forward to seeing him in the morning and at night before she sought out her rest.

Tristan was ever there in her thoughts, a comfort to her soul even when he wasn't beside her.

Was it not better to adore a man who would stand beside her, looking to her as he was now and grant her the love she deserved than to long for a man who had never truly seen her for the woman she is?

"We should return to Summerly," Tristan announced, pinching her chin before he took hold of her hand and pulled her in the direction of their waiting mounts.

Early the following morning Tristan removed his mailed shirt with the aid of his squire, then ran a hand through his damp hair as he made his way from the lists.

He'd pulled himself from the comforts of his bed well before daybreak and spent a good three hours tilting against his squire.

He thought the fresh morning air and a sword in his hands would free his mind of the previous evening, as well as the look in her eyes and the way his palm burned when he touched her cheek.

In the end, he was wrong, he was so distracted that Lance managed to best him a good many times, one of which the squire struck Tristan on the side with such force he feared for a moment that the lad had broken through his chain mail.

"Are you sure you are well?" Lance asked for the third time while he hurried along to keep pace with his master.

"Aye, lad," Tristan assured him. "I will warn you not to let your success in the lists this morning go to your head. I was only distracted with other matters, otherwise you would never have bested me."

"I bested you thrice," Lance reminded, a wide smile stretching across his young face.

"Aye, thrice." Tristan shook his head at his beaming squire.

The lad would be no good to him now. He was positively puffed up with his victory.

Tristan needed to find a way to remove Jocelyn from his mind or it would be he who would be useless. It was then that the laughter of his sisters caught his attention.

He deviated from the course he was taking and followed the sound of their laughter until he was standing on the edge of the garden looking on with amusement.

It seemed Jocelyn was attempting to teach Bethany how to tilt.

They were using sticks for weapons and stood facing one another while Jocelyn delivered a final bit of instruction. His other sisters were scattered about, laughing and cheering with unmasked admiration.

Jocelyn had completely won them over; they were in awe when it came to her. The girls had never been in the company of a lady such as she.

They were told she was grand and important, that was what they expected her to be until Jocelyn arrived dressed as a man. Yet, she took the time to listen to them and offer advice as well as a good amount of her time.

Tristan smiled when Jocelyn advanced and his sister held her ground as she'd been instructed, raising her makeshift sword to ward of her opponent.

"What are they doing?" Lance inquired from where he stood by his master's side, looking on in shock.

"It would seem Lady Artois is teaching Bethany how to tilt," he answered, his eyes fixed on the scene before him.

"Lady Artois knows how to wield a blade? What use has a woman for such a skill?"

"I beg you not to let her hear you say that," Tristan chided with a laugh, "I fear she is powerfully defensive when it comes to her ability to bear arms."

"Tristan!" Norissa called out when she caught sight of her brother looking on. "Look at what Lady Artois taught me!" she exclaimed, bounding toward him, her own stick weapon clutched in her fist.

Tristan smiled warmly at the young girl then glanced to where Jocelyn was now standing beside Bethany, her cheeks kissed by the morning sun, her soft auburn hair escaping the confines of its braid.

He meant to compliment her on her teaching skills when he was taken off guard by his youngest sister striking him bluntly in his stomach with the point of her wooden weapon.

Tristan doubled over and fell to his knees, clutching his stomach as he struggled to catch his breath.

"Oh wonderful!" Norissa shouted with delight. "I never thought it would work so well!"

"Tristan, are you all right?" Jocelyn asked when she knelt down beside him. "Truly I never thought she would do you any real harm," she laughed, patting his back with concern.

"I might accept your apology, if your words weren't laced with amusement," Tristan wheezed. "This is the fourth time I have been bested this morning. I fear you alone are at fault for all my suffering."

"I?" Jocelyn took hold of his arm and helped pull him to his feet. "It was not my doing that you weren't paying attention."

"Aye, sweet Lady, it was." Tristan reached out and pinched her chin before turning to Norissa who was still beaming in triumph.

"As for you, never attack when your opponent's eyes are not on you. Hardly honorable." He took the weapon from the young girl, causing a deep frown to fall over her face.

"Now!" Tristan announced, holding the stick out as he would his heavy sword and pointed the weapon at Jocelyn. "I have a mind to right the wrongs of this morning. "Come lady and prove to me that you are worthy of the sword you carry."

Jocelyn scowled at him for but a second before running back to where she'd dropped her wooden weapon, retrieved it from the ground then turned on him, holding the stick-sword at the ready.

Her lips belied her scowl with a small smile that turned up the corners of her mouth.

"When I best you, it will be five times this day that you have lost the fight and twice to meager girls," Jocelyn taunted, then couldn't help but laugh at his disgusted grunt.

"I will not lose, sweet Lady. I vow it!" With that Tristan attacked and was immediately shocked with her skill.

She was quick on her feet, but that was far from what, shocked him.

Jocelyn matched him blow for blow and the strength in which she delivered her attack was remarkable. He would never have believed a woman of her size could hold such strength.

"I see shock in your eyes," Jocelyn observed, ducking under his stick then turned and smacked him across the back with her own.

"Ouch!" Tristan muttered much to the glee of his sisters, who were looking on from the distance, cheering for Jocelyn to be the victor.

Lance stood beside them, his arms folded, his brows raised in complete amusement.

"My apologies, Sir. Did I cause you great pain?" she teased, backing up a pace or two when he straightened his frame and shook off her abuse.

"Best him Lady Artois, I have never seen anyone best him before!" Anne shouted, from where she stood beside her sisters, clapping her hands and bouncing from foot to foot.

"It seems you have won them over," Tristan mused, advancing on her.

He chose to no longer play it safe, but deliver more challenging blows to find she as well was stepping up her game to match his pace.

"I adore your sisters." Jocelyn jumped back when he struck the wrist of her right hand causing her to drop her weapon.

She shook her abused hand, but made no complaint as she carefully eyed where the stick had fallen and backed away from him while he slowly advanced.

"Careless for you to misplace your weapon, now whatever will you do?" Tristan questioned, slowly stalking her.

"If you were a man of honor, you would return my weapon so the odds might be fair." She eyed him as he reached down and retrieved her fallen stick, holding it captive as he continued to push her deeper into the garden.

"And what if it is not a man of honor whom you fight? What then, sweet Lady?" Tristan asked, pushing to see what she was taught to do in such a situation.

"If we were truly in battle, I would hurl my knife at your rotted heart," Jocelyn informed him, trying to keep her voice free of humor.

"If it failed to hit its mark?"

"It would not, for I am a perfect aim," she stated, tipping her chin up slightly as she continued to move away from him.

"Pride is the devil's curse," Tristan remarked, nearly achieving his goal of backing her into a corner where she would have no choice but to yield.

"As is the arrogance of a dishonorable man."

"In battle, one cannot always uphold his honor," Tristan informed her just as he sensed the presence of someone sneaking up behind him, at the same moment Jocelyn's eyes wavered, focusing on whoever had dared approach him.

"Sword, my Lady," Lance called out; throwing her a stick he'd gained from one of the girls.

"Traitor!" Tristan gasped in mock horror and acted as though he ran the squire through with one of the stick swords he held.

"Oh! I have fallen!" Lance exclaimed to the laughter of Tristan's sisters as he fell to the ground, gripping the stick to his stomach as though he were truly impaled.

"It seems you have won my squire as well. Pity the lad turned on me, the traitor," Tristan accused, hearing Lance laugh with his comment.

Tristan turned back to face Jocelyn and was instantly forced to defend himself against her advance.

"One of the many advantages of being a woman," Jocelyn answered, managing to turn him enough that he was no longer able to back her into a corner.

"Then pray tell, what are the advantages of being a man?" Tristan asked, wincing when she jabbed his shoulder.

"I fear there are none," Jocelyn stated with blunt conviction, then burst into laughter when Tristan stopped dead in his tracks and looked at her as though he was greatly hurt by her words.

"Oh…worry not my dear fellow. That is the reason men need women in their lives. To bring them the advantage they would otherwise never gain."

"Who told you this?" Tristan asked, lifting his weapon again and attacked her so relentlessly she had not the breath to answer him.

He pushed her back, much to the despair of his sisters and it would seem Lance. They were all booing and shouting for her to gain the advantage over her opponent.

Jocelyn ducked and dodged his onslaught, her determination wavering as she struggled to simply remain on her feet.

She saw the gleam of victory in Tristan's eyes and sensed he knew he'd won. Alas, she was determined to show him she was as skilled as any man.

When it seemed she might gain her footing, her stick snapped leaving her nothing but a six-inch remnant she stared at in irritation.

Tristan hesitated for but a moment before propelling her backward, backing her up against the rough stonewall of the keep, placing the stick sword to the tender flesh of her neck and pinned her between himself and the stone.

"I dare say, it is time for you to yield," Tristan announced, holding her captive.

"My father," Jocelyn stated, even as she struggled to catch her breath.

"Your father?" he questioned, fully taken aback by her words.

"Aye, my father. He is the one who told me that it is the woman who brings advantage into a man's life. He has told me many a time that without my mother by his side, he would have nothing. It is not the woman who needs the man, but the man who needs the woman." She bit her bottom lip while she studied the closeness of his face and he contemplated her comment.

"Think you that I need you?" Tristan asked, tipping his head toward her until they were nose-to-nose. "Perhaps it is you who need me?"

His heart was pounding so fiercely as he gazed down into her soft green eyes that he scarcely remembered where he was and who was looking on.

"Are you not going to kiss her?" Norissa called out. "Ouch! Do not strike at me Anne. They have been standing there for an eternity. If he is not going to kiss her, then he should let her go free," Norissa proclaimed.

Tristan shook his head and struggled to stifle an amused laugh.

"Did I not tell you they are constant?" Tristan asked, pulling back a bit.

"Aye, you did." She shook her head, her cheeks turning an enchanting shade of crimson.

"At least my pride is still intact, for I am the victor." He was prepared to take a step back when she reached out, pulled his wooden sword from his hand and held it to his throat.

"Nay, I fear it is you who will yield to me," she announced, beaming at him in victory.

An uproar of shouts rang out from his sisters and Lance who shrugged his shoulders at his master when he was given a glare.

"Say it," Jocelyn ordered with a laugh.

"Never."

"Come now, I deserve to hear you say it," she pleaded, batting her lashes at him.

Tristan took a mighty breath and was prepared to humble himself when a breathless page burst into the garden, pulling them from their merriment with his news.

"Master Tristan, your lady aunt sent me to fetch you. Your father—"

Tristan never gave the lad time to finish; he fled past the page to the yard, up the stairs of the keep, through the great hall to the stairwell that would take him to his father's chamber.

He burst into the room, his chest heaving, his heart faltering as he feared for the inevitable.

He'd told himself he was ready, he knew his father was near the end of his life, but no matter how prepared Tristan thought he was for this moment, he knew it would never be easy.

"Tristan," Mona called out when she took sight of him and stood from where she was kneeling beside her brother's bed.

"He asked for you, I fear it is time." She took hold of her nephews hand and pulled him forward. Her face was streaked with tears as she looked to Tristan with pity.

She knew all that would now be placed on his shoulders and prayed Tristan would be able to bear the weight for all their sakes.

“Father?” Tristan questioned when he came to a stop before the man who raised him.

Mortan was drawn and pale, looking to his son’s eyes as though he had already passed from his life.

“Father, it is Tristan.”

“I know you boy,” Mortan muttered, struggling to open his heavy eyes so he might look at his son. “I have wronged you.”

“Father?”

“I have left you nothing, but debt,” Mortan stated, seeming to know reality for the first time since Tristan returned from Artois.

“I know, Jocelyn and I have studied the ledgers,” he informed him, then resisted the urge to step back when his father’s eyes shot open to look at him with complete clarity.

“Jocelyn…the Lady of Artois…is here at Summerly?” Mortan sputtered before his eyes fell closed once more.

“Aye, you sent me to fetch her. Do you not remember?”

“Heaven forgive me, but I thought it was a dream,” Mortan wheezed then reached out and took hold of his son’s wrist with all the strength that was left to him.

His delusions were real and the nightmare he’d been struggling to free himself from was indeed reality.

“What are you saying?” Tristan questioned, a sense of dread creeping over him when his father stared at him, his eyes hollow and distant.

“I thought she might save us…I thought…Doyle.” His eyes fell closed for he no longer had the will to hold them open.

“Doyle? Father, what have you done?” Tristan sat on the edge of the bed willing him to respond.

“I thought…she might save…us.” The hand that gripped Tristan’s wrist fell limp, dropping to the bed.

His father was gone, but that single fact alone did very little to right the many wrongs he’d committed against his family.

Tristan took a mighty breath as the mystery of Doyle’s name on the ledger became all too clear to his reeling mind.

His father traveled to Artois for one single reason. Mortan was the very same as all the other men who were seeking Jocelyn’s hand. He was in need of her wealth to sustain his floundering holdings.

Doyle was behind the men who ran Jocelyn down in the woods and the reason she had yet to hear from her kin. There was no doubt in his mind Doyle was the reason the men he’d sent to deliver her ring to her father had never returned.

His father sent Doyle to make certain the lady was brought to Summerly, for he had not the faith in his own son to do so.

Tristan leaned forward and rested his head in his hands, silently cursing his father for what he’d done.

How could his father have been so selfish and foolish to take advantage of such a woman?

How was Tristan to tell Jocelyn? How would she ever understand?

Could she ever forgive him?

His aunt's weeping pulled Tristan from his silent misery and back to the dreary reality at hand.

His father was dead, he now had no other choice but to see him buried and his sisters looked after.

Once those matters were seen to, Tristan would return Jocelyn with all haste to her kin and pray it could all be accomplished before Doyle came seeking his payment.

Chapter Twelve

“Stop staring at me,” Rhyes muttered, poking at the snapping embers of the fire with a stick.

“Nay,” Tomas answered from where he sat across from the man, his feet stretched out to the blaze, his arms folded across his wide chest.

“What is it you want with her?” Tomas asked.

He knew his questions would more likely than not lead to heated words then flying fists, but Tomas wanted to know what Rhyes’ intentions were.

“What are yours?” Rhyes answered the question with one of his own.

He had more than just a feeling that Tomas felt a good deal more for his lady than friendship.

“I am the captain of her guard.”

"Nay, you are the captain of her father's guard. I have seen the way you look at her." Rhyes jabbed at the fire, causing a swirl of sparks to leap in the air.

"As I have seen the way you moon over her." Tomas folded his arms a bit tighter and forced himself not to shudder. "You acted as a lovesick pup whenever you were in her company."

"At least I had the courage to voice my affection for her, at least she knew. I would rather be caught mooning than brooding over a woman I will never gain."

"All I would have to do is speak to Lord Milberk, he would grant me her hand if it was his desire to do so," Tomas hissed, even as he knew Robin would never order his daughter to marry any man, no matter what he thought of him.

"Then why do you not ask for her hand?" Rhyes asked, his voice raising slightly.

"Why have you not asked for her?"

"I was asked to speak no such words to her while within her home. I have respected her wishes. Once she is safe, I will waste no time in asking for her hand.

"Unlike you, I have no fear of what her answer will be." Rhyes ducked when Tomas took hold of a handful of dirt and small rocks and hurled it at him.

"Child," Rhyes hissed, loathing the man as he loathed no other.

If it was not for Lord Milberk's order that they remain in one another's company Rhyes would keep as far from the horrid man as was physically possible.

"Oaf," Tomas shot back, his irritation rising.

"Lackwit."

"Wench!" Tomas instantly regretted his insult when Rhyes gained his feet and was upon him in an instant.

"They are at it again," Liza mused from where she sat beside her mother near the fire in the center of the camp.

"I thought we were past their bickering," Robin muttered, rising to make his way across the clearing to put an end to their brawling.

Robin needed both of them alive if they were to retrieve his daughter from her abductors.

"I fear they won't be happy until one of them is dead," Sarah whispered, shaking her head at her daughter as she spoke. "Your father should tie them each to a tree at the opposite ends of camp, then perhaps the rest of us might have a bit of peace."

Sarah stood and followed after her husband, having the feeling that Robin might need her assistance if he was to quiet the bickering without becoming a part of it.

Doyle looked on from where he was posted to stand watch, studying the goings on closely. Lord Milberk broke the two men apart and commenced in reprimanding them for their childish behavior.

He'd come to the conclusion over the past few days that the two of them were ordered to remain together for he could clearly see they detested one another, but were continually in the same company.

He also came to the realization that they were both fighting to win the affection of the very woman they were in route to rescue.

It was a strange predicament to be sure, one that could either work in his favor, or condemn him.

Lord Summerly owed him a fee for his services and he would be had if he was dismissed without what was rightfully his.

He would be paid, and if he needed to use a bit of leverage to gain what was to be his, then so be it. He also owed this irksome Robin of Milberk a bit of his own for the grief he was causing him. He was no man's servant and to be reduced to a minion who stood the night posted as a watchman sparked his temper.

They would pay, he would not leave them be until he personally saw his pains avenged.

Jocelyn held tight to Norissa's hand as they stood before Lord Summerly's grave, the bright midday sun beat down on their heads, the gentle breeze rolled in off the sea as the holy man spoke solemn words of comfort.

She looked to where Tristan stood with his arms folded, his eyes fixed on nothing.

To her, he seemed miles away, fixated with whatever it was that was rolling about in his head.

She'd done her best to help him, but whenever she would approach him, he would find some pressing matter that needed his attention, or ask her to look after one of his sisters.

Jocelyn might blame his distance on the death of his father, but she had a feeling it was something more.

When the burial was complete, she followed the family back to the keep, her hand still gripping Norissa's as it seemed the child refused to let her go.

They stood in the great room for a moment or two before the four older girls retreated to their chamber and were followed shortly after by their weeping aunt, leaving only the three of them to stand in the consuming silence.

Jocelyn allowed her gaze to follow Tristan to the hearth where he rested his hands on the mantle and stood staring into the ashes as though they held the answers his soul was seeking.

"What is the matter with him?" Norissa whispered, her voice littered with tears.

"Everyone wears their grief differently," Jocelyn answered, kneeling down to face the child.

"Will he become like Papa?" she asked, looking past Jocelyn to where her brother was standing.

"What mean you?"

"Papa stood as Tristan is standing now after my mother died. I remember him standing there for hours looking into the hearth, even when there was nothing to see.

"Is that what happens when people die, do you become lost?" the child asked, her deep question etching at her companion's heart.

Jocelyn turned her face from the child to look to where Tristan was standing. He was no longer gazing in to the ashes, but looking back to his sister with glistening eyes.

"Nay, Norissa. Your brother is stronger than that." With that quiet reassurance, the child released her hand and made her way to the stairwell to go in search of her sisters.

"What would you have me do, Tristan?" Jocelyn asked, remaining on her knees where Norissa left her.

"You need to return to your kin," Tristan answered, his voice so low she could barely hear him.

"I feel I am needed here. My family will understand."

"Nay, they will not. Do you not wonder why we have had no word from them? Do you not wonder why the men I sent to Artois have not returned?" Tristan turned his face back to the ashes, too ashamed to look her in the eye.

"I knew not that they were missing." She stood and crossed the distance between them, her mind reeling with questions.

"What is it you are implying?"

"You need to return to your kin and you must do so with all haste," Tristan stated, his words breaking his own heart.

"Why, Tristan?" Jocelyn took hold of his shoulder, begging him to face her.

He stood to his full height and obeyed her silent request, looking down at her with eyes full of an agony she might have blamed on the passing of his father if she knew no better.

"My father betrayed you. He had me bring you here so he might persuade you to wed him. He believed that you alone could mend his past wrongs and grant him the sum he needed to rid Summerly of the debt he owes." His words were low and detached as though he was a world away even though he was standing before her.

"Nay," Jocelyn whispered, hardly able to believe what he was telling her.

"Upon my leaving he hired his favored mercenary to follow me and make certain you were freed of your kin and insure that no one followed after you.

"My father is dead and the man he hired will soon arrive seeking the payment he is owed. You must leave before he arrives to retrieve that which I have not the means to give." He lowered his head and turned back to the hearth, too ashamed to look at her a moment longer.

"You knew why he would have me brought here?" she whispered, her heart aching with the horrid thought that this man she was beginning to love was the same as all the others.

He needed her only for her wealth.

"Nay, I knew nothing of his intentions. Not until moments before he died. I do not expect you to believe me, or forgive what I have done. But, I will make it right. We will leave at first light and return to Artois."

Tristan heard her turn and leave. He heard each of her footfalls as she climbed the stairs and he cursed himself a fool with each and every one.

Tristan loved the woman.

He loved her as he never knew he could love anyone. And because of his father's ill judgment, he was forced to let her go.

She would never see him as the man she once knew. He was changed in her eyes, he was no better than the throng of men she'd forced from her home.

Jocelyn closed the door to her chamber and rested her back against the structure, breathing deeply as she struggled to quiet the rising wave of emotion that was creeping over her.

How could she have let him into her heart?

How could she have been so blind not to see what he was doing?

Alas, Tristan never asked her for anything, never once when they were struggling through the ledgers and writing to postpone payment to those his father owed did Tristan ever imply that she could help him pay off the creditors.

Jocelyn wiped at her eyes and made her way to the clothespress. She pulled her worn tunic and hose from its depths, shrugged out of her borrowed gown and quickly dressed in the men's clothes she'd been wearing when she left Artois.

Once she was dressed, she fastened her sword to her hip and threw her cloak about her shoulders.

As she made her way across the chamber to the door, she tucked her braided hair up under her cap, lifted the latch and entered the dim corridor.

If what he said was true, her family would be sick with worry.

For all they knew, she'd been abducted, taken against her will to suffer a horrid fate.

She could not allow them to worry over her any longer.

In a matter of minutes, she was standing in the stables ordering for her horse.

Much to her surprise, no one tried to stop her when she mounted the beast and made for the wall, where again, she was given no trouble and rode through the gates as she had so many times with Tristan.

She looked back only once, her anger and hurt winning the battle waging in her heart.

She knew the girls would suffer without her. She'd grown to care for them all, even the man who had betrayed her.

Jocelyn had not allowed herself to love since Bart died. She shut her heart to protect it and the moment she allowed herself to give in, she was crushed.

She turned her eyes back to the road ahead and dug her heels in, urging the animal forward.

"Never again," she vowed to herself. Never again would she set herself up for despair.

"Stop weeping," Mary urged her older sister, elbowing Bethany in the ribs before she stood and walked toward the window.

The sun was beginning to set, casting the garden below into shadow.

"You are causing my head to pound," Mary muttered, looking out into the darkening night with a heavy sigh.

“I cannot help it,” Bethany whined, wiping at her eyes with the sleeve of her gown.

“Father would not want us to weep for him,” Millie informed them all, dusting her own tears from her face with the back of her hand.

“Nay, our weeping would drive him mad.” Mary pushed away from the window to plop back down next to where her sisters were huddled together on the window seat.

“Lady Artois said Tristan won’t go mad like father,” Norissa spoke up.

“Hush,” Bethany chided, “what do you know.”

“She told me so, just before I left her with Tristan in the hall,” Norissa defended.

“I want to go find her,” Anne informed them all. Jocelyn always made the day seem a bit brighter; she would pull their minds from their sorrow if she were with them.

“Leave her be. They no doubt have business to attend to,” Bethany ordered, feeling it was her right to do so, she was the oldest after all.

“Nay, I’m tired of listening to you weep.” Anne pushed to her feet and made her way to the door, Norissa following close behind her.

“Think you she will still be in the hall?” Norissa asked, reaching out to take hold of her sister’s hand.

“It is late, perhaps she has gone to her chamber.”

The girls made their way to Jocelyn’s room and knocked lightly on the door then waited as patiently as they were able for her to answer.

When there was no reply, Anne lifted the latch and pushed open the structure to peer into the dim Chamber.

"Lady Artois?" Anne called, but received no answer.

"She is not here," Norissa observed out loud, pushing past her sister to enter the room and look about as if Jocelyn was hiding from her.

"Let us look in the hall, perhaps she is still there with Tristan." They made their way to the hall only to find it terribly dark and deserted.

With tears in their eyes they followed their feet back up the stairs and to the only place left where she might be.

Tristan removed his thick belt and cast it aside along with his sword.

He was weary body and soul.

He'd thought more than once about making his way to Jocelyn's chamber to make certain she was well, but he had the feeling he was the last person she wanted to see at this moment in time.

He would speak to her upon the morrow, if not, it would be a horribly long and silent journey to Artois.

Tristan cursed his foolish father for the hundredth time and flopped down on his bed just as a soft knock sounded against his door.

Tristan forced himself up and crossed the room, pulled open the door to look down at his two youngest sisters.

Their eyes were large and glossy, their hands tightly clasped together.

"What do you up at this hour?" he asked, scowling when Norissa pushed past him into the room and looked about as though she was searching for something she'd lost.

"Oh blast, Anne, but she is not here either," Norissa complained from where she stood in the center of his chamber.

"Who?" Tristan asked, wondering what they were up to.

"Lady Artois. She always makes us feel better. We went to her chamber to find her, but she was not there," Norissa supplied.

"She's not in the hall either," Anne informed him, looking up at her brother with tear-brimmed eyes. "We thought she might be with you."

"Nay, she is not." Tristan reached out and took hold of Norissa's hand, ready to propel her to the door. "Perhaps she has gone for a walk in the garden."

"It is dark out," Norissa complained, looking as though she was ready to burst into tears at any moment.

"Ladies do not walk in the garden after nightfall," Anne assured him, tugging on the sleeve of his tunic as she spoke.

Tristan took a mighty breath and knelt down before them. He was touched that they trusted Jocelyn to the point that they would seek her out to quiet their sorrow, even as the same thought saddened him, for he knew Jocelyn was returning her to Artois in the morning.

"Return to your chamber, I will go and find her."

"Tell her we need her," Anne begged.

"I will not sleep at all if I cannot speak with her," Norissa informed him, the tears that once threatened to fall escaped the confines of her eyes and rolled down her cheeks.

"I will tell her. Now off to bed the both of you, the hour is late." He stood and propelled them out the door before following his feet to Jocelyn's chamber.

He knocked on the door, but there was no answer. He boldly lifted the latch and peered into the room only to find it deserted. He then went to the hall, but it was as his sisters had said, she was not there.

Tristan doubted she would be in the garden, but he went there as well. When he found no sight of her, he stood in the yard, looking to the gate in bewilderment.

She wouldn't be so bold as to leave. He was sure of it, but even so, he made his way to the stables and called for a groom.

"Aye, my Lord," the man answered, running across the building to where Tristan was waiting.

"Have you seen anything of Lady Artois this night?" he asked, his apprehension rising when the man shifted where he stood.

"Aye, near an hour before sunset she came asking for her mount."

"And you gave it to her!" Tristan bellowed, feeling his heart lodge in his throat.

"Aye, my Lord. I was never instructed otherwise." The man extended his hands in apology, clearly sorry for not informing his master of her departure.

"Ready my mount!" Tristan ordered then stalked from the stables.

What could she have been thinking? How could she be so foolish?

He shouted for a page and within moments he was surrounded by fifty or so of his men calling out orders just as his horse was brought to him.

"Ready your mounts and follow after me with all haste," he barked sending the throng of men into motion.

"I would go with you," Lance informed him from where he was standing by Tristan's stirrup.

"I cannot wait for you lad. Give my orders to the Poston. He is to close the gate and let no man enter until I return."

"Aye," Lance answered and was running to the gate even before Tristan put his mount into motion.

Within a matter of seconds, the group was riding through the gate and pounding down the village lanes.

Tristan's anger with Jocelyn's foolishness pushed him forward, as did his terror for her safety. He knew not if Doyle was on his way to Summerly, or if he was still holding her family within the walls of Artois.

Either way, Jocelyn was destined to cross his path sooner or later. He must get to her before that happened, he must keep her safe for it seemed to be his doing that she was in this mess.

It was his responsibility to see her safely returned to her kin.

Chapter Thirteen

Jocelyn drew rein just as the sun was beginning to push up over the horizon.

She dismounted and allowed her mount to drink from the stream that was quietly meandering through the meadow alongside the road.

The sharp edge of her temper was beginning to wear away, leaving in its stead the extreme foolishness of her actions.

She leaned against the side of her horse and contemplated what she should do.

Artois was a good five days ride from Summerly and that was if a person knew where they were going, which she clearly didn't.

The mercenary Tristan's father hired was either still tormenting her family or he was on his way to collect the sum that was owed to him for his pains.

Tristan had surely found her missing by now and would be on his way to fetch her.

Or would he?

She pushed away from the animal and walked into the center of the road, struggling with her pride to make up her mind.

If she continued on she would become lost, or worse. She might stumble upon the band of men Lord Summerly hired to see she was removed from her family.

If she returned to Summerly, she would have to face Tristan.

At the moment, neither of her choices seemed the least bit pleasing.

The sound of riders approaching in the distance pulled her from her frustrations and back to the simple fact that she was a lone woman, a good distance from any who might help her if she was overrun.

She pulled herself up on to her mount and urged him across the stream and into the shelter of the trees. She would have to swallow her pride and return to Summerly. At least she would be safe there until she could be properly escorted home.

Jocelyn remained in the shelter of the trees looking on as a party of fifty or more men, all wearing the colors and bearing the arms of Summerly, passed by on the road.

She scowled at the group, her feelings slightly hurt that Tristan wouldn't come after her himself.

She huffed her irritation with the infuriating man and turned her mount back to Summerly.

What did she expect?

Did she think Tristan would come running after her himself the moment he found her missing?

He claimed to know nothing of his father's intentions, but how could he not? Did he not jump at the man's every whim and remove a woman from her home simply because he was asked?

Tristan had played the whole while as though he was a man who knew nothing of Summerly's plight, feigning to be shocked with the news of his broken inheritance.

He was far from the man she once thought him to be.

Jocelyn ducked under a low branch and let out an annoyed huff with her predicament.

Her father would see him pay for his wrongs of that she was certain.

Against her will, she felt her heart sicken with the sudden thought of what would become of Tristan should her father get his hands on him.

"Good morrow, Jocelyn." The rich tones of Tristan's voice pulled her from her thoughts to the man sitting on his mount before her.

"You?" Jocelyn breathed, struggling to force her heart to not leap with the sight of him.

"Aye, what think you woman to leave the confines of the wall without an escort?" Tristan chastised.

His blunt rebuke caused her cheeks to flame and her feelings toward him to harden once more.

"I only wished to never see you again," she hissed, wanting to have the courage to turn her mount and ride away from him.

He was right in knowing she was foolish for leaving Summerly and he also seemed to know that she needed him, even if it was only for protection.

"Remain alone and you will get your wish for you will surely find yourself dead." Tristan boldly brought his mount forward and took hold of her bridle.

"To be dead would be better than some things in this life," she informed him, pulling roughly upon the reins, causing the confused horse to rear and back away, forcing Tristan to relinquish his hold over her.

"I will not be used for my wealth. Not by you or any man."

"If you think me to be after your wealth you are sorely mistaken." He shook his head at her as he spoke his eyes full of sorrow.

"Do you know me not at all, Jocelyn?"

"Nay. I thought…I thought you were a man of honor. I thought you were different than all the others, but I was wrong. I will return to Summerly for it seems I have no other choice at the moment. But, I want your word that you will return me to my kin and after that moment I never want to see or hear from you again."

"Have you heard nothing of what I have told you?" Tristan asked, urging his mount toward her.

"How could you not know, Tristan? How could you come to fetch me and take me to your father without the slightest knowledge of what you were doing?" Jocelyn questioned, her heart breaking within her chest.

Of all the men who walked into her life of late, why must it be this man who stole her heart?

"Do you desire the truth? I thought the lady my father spoke of to be just that, a lady. I thought when he spoke of the Lady of Artois that she was a grand woman. A woman near his same age, a woman who wore her title with pride, not the ragbag urchin who sits before me now." He ignored her huff and pushed his horse forward until the beast was alongside her own, allowing him to look her in the eye.

"What I found in you, Jocelyn, was someone so much more than what I thought I would find," Tristan stated.

"I have never spoken a false word to you since the moment we met. If you cannot see that, then you are not the woman I know you to be."

"You clearly know nothing of me," she muttered, turning her face from his for fear that he might see the hurt in her eyes.

"Indeed. We have wasted the whole of the day. We will return to Summerly and pass the night. At first light I will escort you to Artois." He turned his mount to the road, never once looking over his shoulder to see if she followed.

Jocelyn remained where he left her, battling with her stubborn pride until he left the concealment of the trees.

What choice did she have?

She would never make it to Artois without him, but even so, she turned the mount toward Artois, opting to face the dangers of the open road rather than look upon him for a moment longer.

She bit her bottom lip in frustration when the sound of him riding after her pounded into her ears.

"What do you?" Tristan asked at a loss, "we will reach Summerly by nightfall if we make haste."

"I travel to Artois," Jocelyn stated, hardly caring that he was growing irritated with her stubbornness.

"We have not the supplies or the escort to make the journey," he informed her, reaching out again to take her reins and force her to comply.

"Nay!" Jocelyn shouted, yanking the reins from his grasp, causing her mount to side step.

"Jocelyn, do not act as a child. You cannot make the journey on your own." He urged his mount forward to match the pace she set, clearly determined not to let her out of his sight.

"I can, and I will. I need not a man," she declared, wishing he would just let her be.

She'd seen his men ride by on the road. If he insisted that she need an escort, they might take her. She had no desire to return to Summerly, not now that she knew what his true intentions had been from the start.

"Do not be so foolish. You think that because you can wield a blade and dress like a man that you are exempt from the frailties of womanhood, you are wrong.

"You are what you are. And I being a man am obligated to see to your safety. I give you no choice, woman! You will return with me to Summerly and you will do so with no further complaint."

Tristan boldly reached out again to gain control of her mount, sparking her temper, not only with his insulting words, but with the harshness in which they were delivered.

Jocelyn dug her heels into her mount, pushing him forward with a shocking burst of speed.

She would rather run than relinquish control to this pompous man.

Tristan was charging after her in a matter of seconds, running her down with relentless speed.

She turned her horse from the trees, leading him through the meadow and back to the road where she might have a better chance in outrunning him.

He had nearly gained on her when she turned her horse again from the road, leading him through the underbrush, across the small meandering stream and into the seclusion of the forest.

She remembered that his men had passed her by only moments before he found her. She had no desire to come across them now that she was running from their master.

Jocelyn ducked under the low branches and struggled to remain in control of her mount, even as she began to regret her decision to leave the road.

Tristan was gaining on her; she could hear the pounding of his horse's hooves as well as the sound of his breath as it escaped his lungs.

She thought of hurling her knife at the lout, but decided against it.

Jocelyn hardly wanted to kill him; she only wanted to be free of him.

"Leave me be!" Jocelyn shouted when he gained on her.

Tristan never answered, but reached out and surprisingly took hold of her about the waist, pulling her against her will from the back of her mount and onto his.

"Now, we return to Summerly," Tristan stated his voice low and full of his victory.

Jocelyn was far from ready to oblige him she elbowed him roughly in the rib and slid from his grasp to land on her feet.

She drew her sword and turned to face him, loathing the amused glint in his eyes.

"Jocelyn stop being foolish," Tristan ordered with a menacing tone that belied the look of amusement on his face.

"I have no desire to go anywhere with you," she informed him, holding her ground when he approached, leading his mount toward her with complete confidence.

"I will not leave you here, take my hand and I will take you to retrieve your mount." He extended his hand to her, clearly thinking she would obey his orders.

"Your hand!" Tristan snapped his fingers at her with his impatience, causing a fire to ignite within her.

"Not if you were the last living being," she hissed, waving her weapon at him.

"If I was the last living being, I would leave you to your own for there would be nothing left to harm you. You will take my hand, woman, or I will have no other choice but to force you, yet again!"

"Touch me and I will run you through!" she threatened taking an involuntary step back when Tristan dismounted and stood to face her.

"Have you gone daft, Jocelyn?" Tristan asked, only adding further fuel to the fire smoldering within her.

"Aye, perhaps I have. Perhaps I have lost the remainder of my wits to even begin to think you were an honorable man.

"How could I have been so blind? How could I have allowed you to hold my heart in your hands? How could I have let you into my soul as I did?

"You tricked me into believing you and now I only wish to be free of you!" she shouted at him, the hold she had on her sword wavering slightly.

Tristan eyed her carefully, realizing then why it was that she was so angry with him.

"Do you love me, Jocelyn?" Tristan asked, carefully stepping toward her only to find that she regained control over her blade and was now pressing the tip of it to his chest with a silent threat that held him at bay.

"Nay," Jocelyn whispered and had it not been for the look of agony in her eyes he might have believed her.

"Riders approaching," Tomas announced, though he had a fairly good idea that the others could see the dust rising up in the distance.

"Men from Summerly," Rhyes mused, noticing at once the colors of their tunics and the insignia sewn to them.

He was ready to put heel to his mount and run the blaggards down when Robin stretched out his hand ordering him to be still.

"They might have word of my daughter, allow them to approach." Robin gave the order for the men that followed behind them to halt.

He, along with Rhyes and Tomas fanned out across the road, blocking it to inform their foe that they sought a word with them. They waited in silence with hands resting on the hilts of their swords as the men advanced.

The group of riders looked slightly apprehensive when they drew closer, but they approached just the same.

"Are you not the father of Lady Artois?" leader of the men inquired before Robin could open his mouth.

"Aye. Where is your cowardly master?" Tomas answered for him, his temper ready to snap.

"For what reason have you sought me out?" Robin asked, urging his mount closer to the grouping of men, desiring answers before Tomas and Rhyes lost what little control that remained to them.

"The lady left the confines of the keep last night we have been searching for her since the wee hours of the morning," the man stated, looking for a moment as though he was relieved that they would no longer search alone.

"Find her!" Robin bellowed, his worry for his daughter heightening to the point of panic.

The men from Summerly were efficiently taken and bound, clearly puzzled by the hostilities being shown toward them. They were offered no answers for their treatment and left behind while their captors went in search of the missing woman.

The army of men Robin brought with him from Artois and Milberk split into groups of twenty, each taking to the task of looking for their master's daughter.

Doyle stood back for a short moment, watching the organized chaos, before offering a few orders of his own to the men that were his.

He'd had all he could stomach of taking commands from this Lord of Milberk. He was beyond ready to be done with him.

He led a group of twelve into the trees and sent the others discreetly off in the direction of Summerly. He was determined to find her first and if that was not the case then he would make his way to Summerly and demand the fee that was owed him.

He'd suffered too greatly on this errand not to be rewarded handsomely for his pains.

Lord Summerly would pay, he would make certain of it.

Rhyes led his group into the trees followed closely by Tomas. The two were fuming as they searched the surrounding area for the woman who was lost.

"We had best find her alive, or it will be your neck," Tomas muttered, keeping his gaze on the passing trees.

Surely if she was there and saw them, she would make herself known.

"Hold your tongue before I remove it," Rhyes hissed, his irritation with his constant companion wearing thin.

"I would like to see you attempt the task, lad." Tomas as well had had his fill of Rhyes and was ready for this affair to be over and done with so that Jocelyn might be safe and Rhyes could be on his way.

"As would I, the silence would be blessed indeed. Why do you not take ten men and search on your own," Rhyes suggested, praying the man would heed his advice.

"For the simple fact that we are ordered to remain together," Tomas reminded him, even as the thought of finding Jocelyn without this man in tow appealed to him. "And I hardly trust you."

"Silence," Rhyes hissed as a faint sound in the distance caught his attention.

It was faint at best, but for all his straining ears could guess, it was a woman's voice rising up in the near distance.

"I hear it as well," Tomas muttered, agreeing with the man for the first time since he'd known him and quietly ordered the men following them to spread out into the trees so they might surround their prey.

When they drew a bit closer, both men quietly dismounted and crept forward, listening as the voices grew louder. They were angry at first, then seemed to lose a bit of the hostility as they conversed.

Rhyes heart began to thump wildly within his chest as he recognized the voice of the woman as Jocelyn's. They found her, he now had the opportunity to free her of her captor and mend his wrongs against her.

"There is but one man," Tomas observed, his voice a low whisper as they crept closer.

"Aye. She seems to have things well in hand," Rhyes agreed.

Both men came to a halt in the shelter of a thick cluster of trees, taking sight of Jocelyn and Tristan standing face to face her sword pointed to his chest.

Tristan's hands were resting at his sides and he seemed for the moment to have no intentions of reaching for his weapon.

"Run him through, Jo," Tomas whispered, from where he was hidden behind a tree, his hand gripping the hilt of his sword.

"Nay!" Jocelyn suddenly yelled.

Her opponent slapped her weapon aside with the palm of his hand then lunged at her.

Tristan yanked her sword from her grasp, but before he could take hold of her, Rhyes and Tomas charged forward, drawing their weapons, ready to fall the man before he could harm her.

Tristan dodged the startling advance, ducking under the first blow then used her weapon to repel the next.

Jocelyn stood dazed for a moment then finally her senses caught up with her astonished mind.

"Rhyes?" she whispered, blinking at the struggling men before her.

It was no shock for her to see Tomas, but a part of her never expected to see Rhyes again, last she knew of him he was dead.

"Stop!" Jocelyn shouted when her shock wore away and she realized it would be Tristan who perished if she didn't intervene.

"Stop this!" she boldly stepped forward when Tristan stumbled.

"Get you back, Jocelyn," Tomas ordered, glancing at her for but a second. "We will end this."

"Nay, do not hurt him!" she pleaded, gaining his full attention.

Tomas turned to face her, leaving Rhyes to battle against the man.

"Have you gone mad?" Tomas asked, scowling at her in bewilderment. "This man stole you away from your home, to hold you as ransom and you would plead for his life?"

"Aye." She pushed past him to where Rhyes and Tristan were struggling, her heart lodged in her throat for fear that she wouldn't be able to stop them.

"Rhyes, Stop!" Jocelyn yelled, begging him to yield.

"Back, Jocelyn!" Rhyes bellowed, his gaze intently fixed on his foe.

"Enough! Tomas, stop him," Jocelyn ordered, turning her plea to Tomas.

"Blast you, Jo!" Tomas cursed and entered the fray.

He shoved Rhyes roughly aside then commenced in seeing to their enemy. The man refused to give in; gripping tightly to his blade, making Tomas's every attempt to free him of it futile.

He finally managed to turn the man so that his back was to Rhyes who in turn stepped forward and clouted him over the back of his head with the hilt of his sword.

Tristan slumped to the ground in a senseless heap at their feet.

"Tristan?" Jocelyn breathed in horror.

She ran to where he lay and fell to her knees beside him. Jocelyn reached out and smoothed her hand down his cheek to his neck making certain he still lived.

"Idiots!" she shouted when her fingers confirmed Tristan's heartbeat. "You might have killed him."

"A thank you for our pains might be more appropriate," Rhyes muttered, reaching down to take hold of her arm and pull her to her feet.

She shook off his hands and shoved him aside, her fear momentarily forgotten by the rekindling of her temper.

"I asked not for your help!" she rebuked, forcing them both to scowl at her.

"He might have killed you," Tomas informed her, his sword still clutched in his hand as he crossed the distance to where she stood.

"He had no intentions of hurting me. He only wanted to return to Summerly until a proper escort might take me home." She looked to Rhyes as she spoke, knowing he would never understand the goings on of the past month, even if she tried to explain it to him.

"That is not what we saw, Jo. He attacked you," Tomas defended.

"Only because I started the quarrel!" she yelled back, of all the time for them to find her, that had been the worst.

She herself had made Tristan look even more as though he was the villain they imagined him to be. She was angry with him, but that did not mean she was in the right to be. Her stubborn pride had now created an even bigger problem to deal with.

"I have been sick with worry over your abduction and yet you attempt to defend the man who is to blame for it," Rhyes muttered, taking hold of her again turning them in the direction of the road, leaving Tomas and Robin's men to see to gathering up the unconscious Tristan.

"I will return you to your father and you can begin your explanation then."

Jocelyn was too exasperated to struggle against him and allowed the fuming man to pull her along beside him.

For an instant, she'd been grateful to see he still lived, but after witnessing his anger toward her, Jocelyn had a feeling her gratitude would be short lived.

Doyle cursed under his breath and waited in silence as the woman was removed from the shelter of the trees and Tristan was hauled off, draped over the back of his mount.

He'd been too late in discovering her whereabouts and in doing so, had missed out on a mighty prize.

He pushed to his feet and motioned for his men to follow. He would make his way to Summerly and finish what he started. He would not be cheated out of what was rightfully his.

Chapter Fourteen

"None of this makes any sense to me," Robin muttered, rubbing at the back of his neck with the palm of his hand.

He looked to the solemn face of his daughter, then to where the man he believed held her against her will was bound and guarded by the stern faced Rhyes and Tomas.

"You would tell me he is innocent?" Robin continued, certain his daughter must be suffering from some kind of delusion, though never once had Jocelyn been dishonest with him in the past.

"Aye, father," Jocelyn readily agreed.

She'd told him the tale Tristan had given her. She'd told him of Lord Summerly's insanity and his ploy to gain her wealth through marriage. Jocelyn also told him that Tristan knew nothing of his plot until moments before his father's death.

Jocelyn told him this to save Tristan's life, not because she believed him to be innocent. She could not see him die at her father's hands.

"I do not understand, Jocelyn. Why did you not contact me and let me know you were well?" Robin folded his arms and studied her carefully, noting a difference in her though he knew not what it was.

"I sent you my ring when I first met Tristan and a missive after I arrived at Summerly. I can only guess it was intercepted by the man Lord Summerly hired to keep you from following after me.

"I was never held against my will, I give you my word. Nor was I taken by force to Summerly. I traveled there to see an aged lord whom I believed was my friend." She glanced for but a second to where Tristan was being held, hating the agony in his eyes and the helplessness of his current situation.

Doyle and his men had been found missing, she knew as well as Tristan where the man was headed, as well as the havoc that would be wrought if Tristan wasn't there to stop him.

"You would have me free him?" Robin asked, his heart still fighting with the tale she'd fed him.

"Aye, let him return to his family."

Jocelyn watched her father nod, then hesitantly turned from her to cross the short distance to where Tristan was being detained.

Robin stood there for a moment studying the man, as he seemed to consider what should be done.

"My daughter has granted you your life, Tristan of Summerly," Robin stated, holding the man's gaze with his own. "Though I have a feeling there is more to the tale than she has given me. Even so, I give you back your freedom. Return to your kin."

"Lord Milberk?' Rhyes questioned, clearly seeking justice for the crimes committed.

"Free him and his men; this is now out of my hands." Robin turned to leave, taking hold of Jocelyn to lead her into the camp where her mother and sister were anxiously waiting for her.

Tristan watched her go as the thick ropes that bound him were roughly removed.

She'd saved his life with nothing less than the truth, but he could see she was still far from believing it.

"Retrieve your men and get you from here," Rhyes ordered, shoving Tristan in the direction of his men.

"I have done nothing wrong. You of all should know me better," Tristan informed him, struggling to keep a tight hold over his anger. This was far from the place to lose control.

"Were we not once friends you and I?" Tristan asked, his feeling of contempt for the situation that surrounded him sounding in his voice.

"That was many years ago. It would seem time has changed us both." Rhyes drew his sword and watched as Tristan freed his men, ordering them to fetch their mounts and be on their way.

"You are wrong. Time has changed us very little. You are still the hotheaded brute you always were." Tristan took hold of his horse and pulled himself up into the saddle, ignoring Rhyes obvious irritation with him when he looked to where Jocelyn was conversing with her kin.

She glanced up at him for but a moment, meeting his eyes with her own.

Tristan nodded his gratitude for there was nothing else he could do from this distance. His thanks given, he turned from the camp, following his men back up the road in the direction of Summerly.

Doyle had a good head start and if Tristan wasn't there to stop him, there was no knowing the devastation the man would reap in his absence.

"I am well," Jocelyn assured her mother for the sixth time and pushed to her feet.

She was tired of their questions and was rapidly losing the battle she was waging with her conscience.

It would be well near midnight before Tristan reached Summerly, by then, Doyle might have already breached the wall and taken the castle.

What would become of his sisters and aunt if that happened?

She walked away from the fire she'd been sharing with her mother and sister and followed her feet to the stream at the far end of the camp.

Jocelyn closed her eyes against a sudden onslaught of tears and fought to control her emotion. She'd not been raised to stand aside and allow those whom she loves to suffer.

In truth she loved him, it mattered not who he was or where he hailed from, nor the crimes she believed Tristan and his father committed against her.

She'd been taught to honor family and friendships, for they were the alliances that would last and lift her up when it was her who was in need.

Jocelyn loved him, even if it was against her will.

"Jocelyn?" Rhyes rich voice reached her ears.

His approach caused her to wipe at her eyes and straighten her shoulders to pretend that all was well. The last thing she needed now was for him to see her weeping.

"Your mother asked me to make certain you are well." He came to stand beside her, his eyes scanning over the dimming forest.

"I have told her she has no need to fear, I am only weary." Jocelyn hugged her shoulders and shifted her feet where she stood.

"It has been a long month for your kin, Jocelyn, they have been suffering with the agony of not knowing," Rhyes informed her softly.

"I am well," Jocelyn snapped, wiping with irritation at her eyes.

"Are you?" Rhyes asked with deep concern. Everyone could see she was struggling still.

"Aye," she cried, losing the battle with her fear and sorrow and could do nothing else but let the tears roll down her cheeks.

"It is not I whom my mother should be concerned for this night. If my mother should worry, it should be for those who will surely suffer because of my foolishness."

"You have done nothing wrong," Rhyes assured, placing his hand on her back.

The touch of his hand caused her flesh to burn with the memory of a similar gesture, a gesture offered freely by the man who held sway over her heart.

"Leave me be," Jocelyn whispered, shrugging off his touch.

"Jocelyn, I have things to discuss with you." He took hold of her arm when she made to leave him, clearly determined to speak with her.

"Nay," Jocelyn answered, not having the resolve to speak with him this night, for she had an inkling she knew what it was he wished to discuss.

"I am thankful you live, for I once thought you to be dead. I am grateful to you for helping my family." Jocelyn tried to push past him, but he held her firm.

"I would love you Jocelyn, if you would but give me the chance," Rhyes stated, pleading with her to listen.

"You *would* love me?" Jocelyn questioned, her temper rising with his words.

"There was a time I might have considered you, but that time is past. My heart no longer harbors the ability to love you in the way you would have it, Sir."

"Jocelyn," Rhyes began, only to be cut short by Tomas who stepped from the darkness determined to free her of Rhyes' unwanted advices.

"I fear she has spoken, *friend.* It is time to honor her wishes," Tomas informed him, extending his hand to Jocelyn.

"Would you bid for my hand as well?" Jocelyn asked of him, her eyes welling up with fresh tears.

She pushed past both Tomas and Rhyes and turned to face the stunned pair when she was out of their reach.

Jocelyn was determined to end this foolishness once and for all.

"Would you fall to your knees and vow your never ending love for me? Would you tell me it is I whom you love and not my title or the magnificent holding I would bring you?

"If I had naught but the ragged clothes on my back, would the two of you remain before me, fighting for my hand though I had nothing to offer you but myself?" Jocelyn yelled, causing the eyes of the entire camp to fall on them.

"Nay, you would not! I would be nothing to you then and so I am nothing to you now. I beg you both to leave me be." Jocelyn shook her head at their hurtful silence and stalked away.

"Well done," Rhyes muttered to his companion.

"Havc you not ears? She was addressing you as well. You might have opened your mouth instead of standing there as a muted fool," Tomas answered.

"What is a man to say to the face of such anger? I lose all wit in the presence of tears." Rhyes folded his arms and shook his head, a thousand thoughts of what he should have said rolling about in his mind.

"Aye, it would seem we have both been rejected," Tomas mused, loathing himself for being a fool. Jocelyn was dear to him and yet he'd let her down, he was no better than all the others.

"Aye, so it would seem," Rhyes agreed.

"Father," Jocelyn called out as she ran through the camp, determined to quiet her nagging conscience.

"What was that about?" Robin asked, though he had a pretty good feeling he knew the answer to his own question.

"Twits, the both of them," she muttered, then quickly changed the subject.

"I need to help Tristan," she informed him, caring not if he refused to help her. She would take the men from Artois and go herself. She could not stand by and do nothing.

"What mean you?" Robin asked, following after Jocelyn when she made for the makeshift stables at the far end of camp.

"His father hired Doyle to make certain I was taken to Summerly. The foul man has clearly made his way to the keep intending to claim his fee.

"Lord Summerly is dead and Tristan is hours behind him. I cannot dare to think of what will happen to Tristan's family if Doyle gains entrance to the keep." She called for her horse and gave orders for her men to be brought to her.

"Tristan will have to pay that which his father owes the man," Robin stated, still not understanding why she was so adamant about risking her own safety for the sake of this man.

"There is nothing left to Summerly, the keep is all but destitute." Jocelyn pulled herself up into the saddle praying he would help her.

"Let him fight his own battles, Jocelyn, this no longer concerns you. You owe him nothing." Robin took hold of her horses bridle willing her to reconsider.

"You raised me better than that. I cannot, in good conscience, stand aside and know innocent people are suffering.

"What good is it to possess wealth and a powerful garrison if I do not use them for good?

"I will do this without you, father." Jocelyn searched his eyes as the commotion of men readying their mounts and saddling up pierced the peaceful night air.

"Tristan of Summerly is still a villain in my eyes, love. I cannot aid you, not in this." He shook his head at her and took a step back.

Jocelyn nodded her silent agreement and turned her mount, ready to give the order to ride out when her eyes fell on Tomas and Rhyes, mounted up before her and ready for battle.

"What are you about?" Jocelyn asked, her brow furrowed in a scowl.

"Am I not your captain?" Tomas answered, his tone deep and matter of fact.

"I am ordered, by your own father, to remain by this lout's side." Rhyes shrugged, then seemed to smile at Tomas who answered his grin with a nod. "I have no choice but to go with him."

"Louts the both of you," Jocelyn murmured, slightly bewildered with their sudden friendship.

"Give the order to leave, we make all haste to Summerly," she ordered to Tomas and gave one final look to her father, hoping he would reconsider.

Tomas quickly obliged her and within a matter of seconds they were galloping down the road toward Summerly.

"What has happened?" Sarah asked of her husband when she joined him to see her daughter riding off into the night.

Liza was running across the camp to where her mother and father were now standing, watching as the last of Artois' men thundered past.

"Where are they going?" Liza questioned, her voice low and breathless from her run.

"They ride to Summerly," Robin answered, his guilt beginning to rise up within him.

"Why?" Sarah breathed, hardly believing Robin would allow Jocelyn to leave without him.

"To prevent Doyle from taking the keep. She's gone to help the man who abducted her." Robin shook his head with his daughter's foolishness, even as he struggled to ignore his wife's penetrating glare.

"Yet here you stand, her father?" Sarah asked, completely shocked with her husband's lack in compassion for those in need.

Sarah was right and Robin knew it, he could not stand aside and let their daughter face this alone.

Jocelyn clearly had a reason for feeling as she did, and even though he knew not what it was, he could not stand aside.

"Robin?" Sarah shouted, knowing if they were to catch up with her they needed to leave at once.

"Ready the men!" Robin bellowed into the night before turning and kissing his wife soundly on the forehead, he then ran past her to see to the gathering of his men.

Lance bolted the door to the lady's solar then turned and looked about the room for anything that might be used as a barricade.

Mona seemed to sense what it was he was looking for and flew into motion.

"The table lad," Mona suggested, then commenced in helping him haul the heavy piece of furniture across the chamber to the door. "Girls, fetch the trunk and chairs, hurry now."

In a matter of moments, they managed to barricade the door as best they could, then stood in the eerie silence as the sound of the battering ram beat against the outer wall.

The gate had been ready to give when Lance burst into the keep ordering them upstairs.

He knew not what was keeping Tristan, but he found himself eagerly praying his master would return with all haste.

The watch had seen Doyle and his men approaching, they'd seen him, but hardly expected him to attack with such a wild anger when the gates remained closed to him. They showered him with arrows from above, but his army was relentless, beating against the closed gate with such determination and power that it began to split and buckle after the first handful of blows.

"Where is Tristan?" Bethany whispered in horror when the unmistakable sound of battle filled the courtyard bellow.

She was huddled in the far corner, holding tightly to her younger sisters.

"He will come," Norissa assured them, her body shaking violently from her paralyzing fear.

"He has gone to bring Lady Artois back," Mary whispered, her voice quivering as she spoke. "He knows not that we are in danger."

"Hush," Lance ordered briskly from across the room where he was standing by the door, his sword drawn, his ears straining to hear any threat from the other side of the door.

He alone was not enough to protect them if the door was breeched, but he would give his life trying to see that the kin of his master remained safe.

It was well past midnight when Summerly came into view upon the horizon.

Tristan let his breath out in an infuriated hiss when he beheld the sight of the village set ablaze against the darkness.

They were too late, Doyle had fallen upon Summerly determined to reap his revenge for the contract made with his father.

He pushed his mount forward, his heart longing to know that his sisters had suffered nothing more than fear.

They thundered through the broken gate and entered the fray, doing all they could to help his men free the keep of the ruthless army of mercenaries.

Chapter Fifteen

Jocelyn brought her mount to a rearing halt when she caught sight of the fires blazing in the distance.

"The village," she whispered more to herself than to the men on either side of her.

"Perhaps you should stay behind," Rhyes suggested, instantly regretting his words for the look she gave him might have melted ice. "Very well, lead on, Lady."

"One day," Tomas muttered, shaking his head at Rhyes. "One day you will discover that she is unlike other women and then you will show her the respect she deserves. Remain behind? That is the most idiotic drivel I have ever heard pass through your lips."

"What is she to do but get herself killed? You are the captain and you said nothing," Rhyes scolded.

"I know better," Tomas retorted.

Jocelyn ignored the two men and urged her mount forward, approaching the smoldering rubble that was once the thriving village.

All the work she and Tristan had done the past month was now nothing, but fire and ash.

The hope she once had for Summerly to gain its feet seemed no more.

How could they recover from this trial and so late in the season?

They would have nothing to sustain them through the winter, let alone fulfill the promises of payment to those whom Summerly owed.

There was no sign of life, telling her the villagers had fled for their lives, deserting their homes in the hope to escape with their lives rather than their earthly possessions.

Jocelyn drew her blade when the unmistakable sound of battle shattered the night air. She swallowed the lump in her throat as the crumbled remnants of the gate filled her view.

Doyle had gained access to the yard.

Tomas shouted the order to advance, bringing her small army through the gates to meet the enemy head on with a force that she prayed would be enough to bring Doyle's minions to their knees.

Jocelyn searched the frantic yard for any sign of Tristan, but for all her searching, he was nowhere to be found.

She could tell at first glance that Summerly's men had taken a beating. In spite of their masters warning, they were not ready for such an attack and had lost a great many men because of it.

The two men who rode beside her were relentless in bringing down their foe before any had a chance to reach her, granting Jocelyn the opportunity to continue her search for Tristan.

It was not even moments later when the sky was beginning to brighten with the promise of morning that she caught sight of Tristan, struggling in the distance.

He was being held at bay near the base of the stairs fighting against two men who seemed determined to block his way.

Jocelyn put heel to her horse, urging the animal closer to the struggling men. In a swift movement and nearly without thinking, she pulled her knife from her belt and hurled it at one of his enemy, striking the man just as he lifted his sword and was ready to deliver a blow that might have ended Tristan's struggle.

Tristan shoved his remaining opponent back, catching sight of her sitting upon her mount just behind him. He scowled at her for a moment in clear bewilderment, then was forced to defend himself once more.

The battle seemed to constrict around them, closing them off from the remainder of the open yard where the majority of her men were fighting.

Rhyes and Tomas were now on foot fighting as Tristan was to gain access to the keep.

"Jocelyn," Tristan called out, managing to gain her attention.

She looked to him, instantly seeing the agony in his eyes and knew what it was he would ask of her.

"I have seen nothing of my sisters!" Tristan shouted, glancing momentarily to the door of the keep before turning his full attention back to the battle at hand.

"I will find them!" she vowed, pushing her horse to the steps of the keep. She dismounted and was running up the stairs two at a time before anyone had the chance to stop her.

"Blast it woman!" Rhyes shouted, struggling to free himself and follow after her. But for all his efforts, he remained where he was, fighting a battle he was beginning to fear might not be won.

He glanced to Tomas, clearly seeing his own anger and frustrations at not being able to go with her.

Jocelyn burst into the hall, instantly finding it deserted and deathly silent.

She held tightly to her sword and struggled to breathe as she ran across the trampled rushes to the stairwell that would lead her to the upper levels of the keep.

She remembered vividly Mona telling her that when Doyle and his men were within the walls of Summerly, she would lock herself and the girls in the lady's solar until he was no longer a threat to them.

Jocelyn pounded up the stairs and ran down the corridor, coming to a breathless stop before the door and lifted the latch, breathing a sigh of relief when she found it locked.

"Are you there?" Jocelyn called out, returning her sword to its sheath and knocked again before resting her forehead against the structure. "It is Jocelyn."

Doyle looked on from the shadows of the stairwell watching as she placed her head against the door, willing it to be opened to her.

He'd been hidden away in the study, ransacking the place, searching for anything that might prove useful to him.

Once he gained entrance to the hall, he ordered his men to prevent anyone from entering after him. It would seem she slipped through the cracks.

Perhaps he'd found something of use after all.

"It is Lady Artois!" Norissa shouted, breaking free of her sisters to run to the door. "She has come to help us!"

Lance heaved back the furniture that blocked the door then lifted the bolt and pulled the structure open, allowing her to enter.

Jocelyn flew into the room and was instantly smothered by the group of weeping girls who clung to her as though she'd fallen from heaven as the answer to their prayers.

"Is Tristan with you?" Mona asked, her voice tight with her anxiety.

"Aye, he is struggling to gain control," Jocelyn answered, doing her best to quiet their fears.

"You are all here?" she asked, pulling back to take a closer look at each of the girls.

"I knew he would come," Norissa announced, her voice filled with pride.

"We must get you to safety," Jocelyn began, turning them to the door, but stopped cold in her tracks, for the doorway was blocked by a towering, black haired man.

"I fear you will come with me now, Lady Artois," Doyle instructed, raising the crossbow he held, pointing it, not at her, but to where Bethany was standing frozen beside her aunt.

"You will not take her," Lance stated, stepping before Jocelyn, his sword raised in determination.

Doyle never hesitated and let his arrow fly, striking the young woman in the shoulder, causing Bethany to fall to the floor with an outcry of pain.

"That was a warning lad, it was an intentional miss," Doyle sneered, reloading his crossbow with lightning speed.

"Step aside," Doyle ordered, pointing the weapon again to the grouping of young women who were now huddled around their fallen sister.

"Look after Bethany," Jocelyn softly ordered, pushing Tristan's squire aside to approach the threatening man she could only assume was Doyle.

"Bold Lady, very bold." Doyle reached out and grabbed hold of her arm the second she was close enough.

He pulled her roughly out into the corridor and dragged her down the stairwell before coming to a halt in the vacant hall.

"It is now time to strike a bargain, you and I," Doyle informed her, turning Jocelyn to face him.

He was gripping her arm so tightly she feared for a moment that she would never again regain feeling in the limb. Alas, that was the least of her worries.

Tristan fought against his enemy, joining forces with the men who once threatened his own life.

He knew not why she came back.

Tristan only knew he was grateful for her. He as well as his men would surely have fallen by now.

They were still struggling to gain the advantage, but he could slowly see Doyle's men falling back, it would not be long before control was gained and they could finally end this.

A deep thunder rose up in the distance, pounding fear into the hearts of the mercenaries and granting hope to those who fought to defend the keep.

Tristan felt a smile of relief cross over his mouth when Lord Milberk burst into the yard, bringing with him his garrison and victory.

"Where is Jocelyn?" Robin shouted at Tomas and Rhyes when he was able to make his way to the base of the stairs where the three of them finally managed to be free of their enemy.

"She went within," Tristan answered, nodding his thanks to the man before turning to the stairs.

Tristan charged up the stairs, longing to know his sisters were safe as well as the woman who helped bring victory to Summerly.

Doyle released Jocelyn, but only after roughly slamming her against the wall, pointing his crossbow at her heart.

"Tell me woman, what sort of wealth have you to offer a man such as myself?" he asked, tipping his head at her as he spoke.

"None," Jocelyn answered, her heart thumping so loudly in her ears she feared it might deafen her.

"I know better. You were brought here for the sole purpose of saving this floundering holding. I know, for it was I who was sent after Mortan's fool son to ensure the man could fulfill the task. Perhaps, if the whelp knew of the full extent of his father's idiocy, he would have sought after you himself."

Jocelyn scowled at his words and remained silent, allowing Doyle to unknowingly answer all the questions she had concerning Tristan's involvement in her abduction.

"If Tristan had known what you could do for the keep, his father has so foolishly destined to ruin, he would have journeyed to Artois and brought you back as his own," Doyle laughed at Tristan's lack in knowledge and took a step closer to her.

"I will take Summerly as the fee that is owed to me by Mortan and you have the means to make my suffering at your father's hands worth my while."

"I will do nothing of the sort," Jocelyn stated, knowing she was of far more worth to him alive than dead. He would not harm her, not as long as she was of use to him.

"There is a roomful of leverage upstairs, or have you forgotten. They have gained your compliance once and if needs be they will do so again," Doyle threatened, acting as though he would pull her to the stairwell when the door to the hall burst open, filling the space with the men who consumed her life.

Doyle took hold of her, placing her between himself and his enemy. Using her as a human shield, he pointed his crossbow at her back, the tip of the arrow stabbing her flesh.

"Aw Lord Milberk, come to the aid of your enemy I see," Doyle taunted, easing them away from the wall and into the center of the room.

"I have come for my daughter," Robin stated, wishing he'd been with her from the beginning.

"It would seem you are too late. I have a debt to settle with the woman." Doyle held tight to her arm, refusing her any amount of hope for freedom.

"The debt you have to settle is with me," Tristan announced, his pale green eyes intently fixed on the threat before him.

"Aye, you are terribly wise to assume my debt is unsettled with you. You will pay, mark my word, but who will pay for the days of forced service I suffered under the command of Lord

Milberk?" Doyle questioned, turning his venom on Robin.

"You suffered only that which you deserved," Rhyes informed him, his anger near a breaking point.

Rhyes knew no good would come from Jocelyn returning to Summerly. They should have remained on the road, making their way back to Artois.

"You…" Doyle sneered, his eyes falling to the man who was responsible for all his recent grievances.

Doyle lifted his crossbow and fired, falling Rhyes with a blow to the heart.

"I should have killed you the first time I saw you," Doyle cursed.

"Rhyes!" Jocelyn screamed, looking on in horror as the man lay motionless on the floor.

She struggled against her captor, willing herself to be free.

Doyle dropped the now useless crossbow replacing it with the knife he wore on his belt.

"You will be still!" he ordered, causing her skin to crawl. "I suggest we begin to lay down some terms to our treaty, the sooner we all come to an agreement the sooner she goes free."

"What makes you believe you will leave this place alive?" Tomas asked from where he was kneeling beside Rhyes, his hand resting on the man's shoulder, his anger and anxiety causing his vision to blur until all he saw was the death of the loathsome man who was holding Jocelyn hostage.

"Have you not eyes man, I hold all I desire at my fingertips. You will never lay a hand on me as long as she is in my possession." Doyle shook Jocelyn roughly as if to make his point, causing every one of the men standing before them to bristle.

Tristan glared him down, wanting nothing more than to go back to where this mess began and right the foolish choices he'd made in the past. Choices that now affected each and every one of them.

"As for you, Lord Summerly," Doyle mused, nodding to Tristan, an amused smile parting his lips. "I will take this bedraggled keep off your hands as the payment you owe me. And my dear Lord Milberk, I fear the humiliation I suffered at your hands will cost you greatly. Twice what I might have been paid by Mortan the fool will be what you owe me. Until I have the sum in my hands your daughter will remain with me."

"Nay!" Tristan announced, slashing his hand through the air in denial as he spoke. "Keep Summerly if you will, but Jocelyn goes free."

"How will I ensure possession of that which is mine if I have no collateral? Summerly is yours to barter as you will, but I fear as far as the woman is concerned, you have no say in this. Unless you would choose to leave one of your dear sisters behind," Doyle mused, gaining the desired effect on the man before him. "Perhaps the one with my arrow protruding from her shoulder would be sufficient."

Tristan's eyes fell on Jocelyn, causing her to shudder with the sheer agony they held.

"Bethany," she whispered, answering his silent question, then feared her answer did little to help him.

"This will end! It will end with your blood on my sword," Tristan vowed, taking a risky step forward.

"Bold words spoken by the mouth of a fool. Do you desire her dead?" Doyle shouted, pulling the knife from her back and placed the weapon to her neck where it was a visual reminder of what they had to lose.

Tristan stopped in his tracks, his heart beset with agony. His beloved sister was injured somewhere in the keep and the woman who held his heart stood before him, helplessly teetering on the edge of her life.

"Agree, Lord Milberk and I will spare your daughter's life. Return to your keep and fetch the coin and return. Once I have that which you owe in my grasp, I will set her free. You have my word."

Robin held his ground, his mind determined to find another way. It would be weeks before he could make his way back to Milberk and another fortnight or more to return to Summerly, he could not leave Jocelyn here for near on a month.

This would not be.

"What say you, my Lord?" Doyle asked, clearly becoming impatient with Robin's hesitation.

"I seem to have little choice in the matter," Robin breathed, his eyes falling to the face of his daughter. "But if this is to be, then it will be as I say."

"State your terms and we shall see," Doyle ordered, his mouth twisting into a smile with the thought that he was so close to gaining that which was rightfully his.

"I will not leave her behind with this man," Tristan whispered, his voice filled with his irritation with their situation.

"Neither will I," Tomas agreed from where he was still kneeling beside Rhyes. "We can easily overtake him," Tomas whispered.

"His men are taken, there is no one left to him. If we could get her away from his grasp for but a second that would be all we need." Tristan shifted where he stood, knowing if Doyle released her for only a moment, the fiend would be done for.

"I know what you plot," Doyle hissed, pulling Jocelyn slowly across the hall toward the kitchen and the only exit left to him. "It will not work."

"We plot only the quickest way to return to Milberk," Robin lied.

They had very little time to act. Doyle was becoming desperate, the longer they wavered, the more dangerous it became for Jocelyn.

Robin nodded to Tomas, bringing the man to his feet and out the door.

"Go with him," Robin ordered to Tristan. He knew the keep far better than Tomas; he would be able to get them back in as efficiently as possible.

"What are they about?" Doyle questioned, tightening his grip on the woman as he nervously shuffled his feet.

"Think you I would leave my daughter alone with you?" Robin answered, raising his hands as though his intentions were purely innocent.

"You expect us to stand here for the whole of a month and wait for them to return from Milberk," Doyle muttered, clearly thinking the man to be daft.

"Aye, perhaps you should make yourself comfortable for I fear it will be a long, tedious month." Robin folded his arms and glared him down.

Jocelyn searched her father's face, but his stern features gave very little away.

She had a feeling Tomas and Tristan were not on their way to Milberk. Her father would never be so foolish. She had no choice at the moment, but to bide her time and pray that whatever they were plotting would work.

"Surely there is an outer door leading to the kitchen." Tomas bounded down the outer stairs, Tristan close on his heels.

He was none too sure of this man's intentions with Jocelyn, but he had little choice now but to trust him.

"Aye, this way." Tristan led them through the chaos of the yard, and along the side of the keep and into what remained of the trampled gardens.

As Tristan beheld the tattered remnants of his home, there was no doubt in his mind that Summerly was in ruin.

It would take little more than a miracle to mend what was done. Repairing damage such as this would take a small fortune. A small fortune that might as well be the king's own treasure.

"Once we gain the kitchen, there are two entrances to the hall, one near where Doyle was standing and the other to the rear of the hall," Tristan informed Tomas just as they came to a halt at the broken door that led to the kitchen.

"If one of us distracts him at the far end of the hall, the other might make use of the door closest to him and do away with the foul man before he has a chance to cause Jocelyn harm," Tomas suggested, his voice a thick whisper.

"Which door do you choose?" Tristan asked, more than ready to rid the world of the man who had succeeded in destroying his home.

Tomas hesitated for a moment, studying Tristan carefully before he spoke.

"What is she to you?" Tomas shook his head when Tristan scowled at him and then rephrased the question. "Jocelyn, tell me truly, is the tale she told her father true, or was she merely granting you your life because she has a soul?"

"It is true. I knew not what my father intended when I traveled to Artois. Had I known I never would have made the journey," Tristan informed him with conviction.

"What is she to you?" Tomas asked again, knowing this time his question would be understood.

"I would ask the same question of you, Sir."

"I love her," Tomas stated without hesitation, "as did Rhyes. She refused us both and now I ask you, what is this woman worth to you?"

"My life," Tristan answered, his voice thick and low.

"The first door is yours, I will take the second." Tomas clasped his hand on Tristan's shoulder then stepped past him and through the door.

Without a moment of hesitation, Tomas entered the kitchen, minding his footing as he crept to the far end of the room then waited to act until Tristan was ready.

He looked to the man with envy, knowing once this was over, Tristan of Summerly would acquire everything he himself longed for.

Tomas had seen the way she looked at the man. He'd heard her speak what she believed was a lie to her father to save him, and then he beheld the agony in her eyes and heard it in her voice when she knew he was suffering and she was doing nothing to help him.

Jocelyn loved him.

This was what Tomas had told himself she deserved all along. This was the only way he could step aside and know she would be well.

Tristan nodded to Tomas once he reached the doorway and was ready.

Tomas took a mighty breath and stepped from his concealment, praying their plan wouldn't go amiss and they would have nothing more to regret once this day was over.

"I cannot believe that you sent them to your holding!" Doyle bellowed.

His anger filled voice drowned out the faint sound that caused Jocelyn's heart to still. It was the snap of the rushes, telling her someone was coming up behind them.

Robin's eyes never faltered, not once did he give any hint that Doyle's reign over them was nearly over.

"Believe what you will, I refuse to leave," Robin stated, tightening his folded arm, his eyes belying the fact that he could clearly see Tomas carefully creeping toward his enemy.

"What have you done?" Doyle hissed, tightening his grip on his captive.

"I have done nothing," Robin answered, placing his daughter's very life in the hands of others as he watched Tomas deliberately knock over one of the chairs surrounding the table.

Doyle spun on his heel, his eyes wide with shock, his resolve snapping with the sight of his enemy mere paces from where he stood.

He reached down and pulled the woman's sword from her belt, released the hold on her and turned to face his foe. Doyle hurled the knife he once held against her neck at Tomas just as Tristan came barreling out the door behind him.

Tristan gave him no time to respond, pushing Doyle back with blow after relentless blow, forcing him across the spacious hall until he had nowhere left to run.

"You have destroyed my home!" Tristan bellowed, his voice laced with rage. "Injured my sister and assaulted the woman I love. I am done with you!"

Jocelyn gained her feet and rushed to where Tomas had fallen, longing to find him alive.

She knelt down beside him, sobbing with alarm when he pushed her hands aside and sat up clutching his side where the knife had pierced his flesh.

"It is nothing, cease your weeping, I am well," Tomas ordered, pulling her into his arms when the deafening clang of steel in the distance fell silent.

Jocelyn clung fiercely to Tomas until the quiet of the hall pushed into her thoughts, only then did she pull away from the shelter of his embrace and turn to where Tristan stood across the hall.

His head was lowered, his back to her as he looked to the fallen man before him.

It was done. Doyle would never again be a threat to his family.

"Swallow your pride and go to him," Tomas muttered pushing her away from him. "The fool man believes he loves you, of all women."

"My thanks, Tomas," Jocelyn whispered wrapping her arms once again about his neck before pushing to her feet.

Slowly, Jocelyn crossed the distance to where Tristan stood motionless, hesitating for only a moment.

"Tristan?" she whispered so low she was afraid he didn't hear her.

“Aye,” Tristan answered, turning to face her, his agony leaving his eyes the moment he looked upon her.

“Forgive me,” Jocelyn breathed, wanting nothing more than to let him know at once that she’d been terribly wrong. “I was a fool,” she sobbed, her heart crushing under the weight of her regret.

Tristan dropped his sword to the ground and reached out to pull her into his arms, clinging to her as she did to him, vowing to never let her from his sight again.

Tristan cared not what he must do to be worthy of her. He would find a way, for he now knew he would never be whole without her.

Chapter Sixteen

Jocelyn looked out over the yard, her eyes taking in the disarray that followed the aftermath of such a frightening ordeal.

The men who were once fighting were now seeing to the wounded and struggling to find some balance of order amidst the chaos.

There was no denying the fact that Summerly was in ruin.

The village was completely gone, the gate was in shambles. The barracks were burnt to the ground and well beyond salvaging. Though the stables were still standing as well as the chapel, they had taken a severe beating. Every door had been broken in, every window shattered and every bit of vegetation that once thrived in the garden was trampled beyond recognition.

“She will make a full recovery,” Sarah informed her daughter, startling Jocelyn out of her thoughts.

Sarah had seen to Bethany's wound and did her very best to quiet the fears of the other girls. Assuring them there was no one left to cause them harm.

"My thanks." Jocelyn laced her arm through her mother's and took a mighty breath.

"It is gone," Jocelyn whispered, "Summerly was struggling before. I know not how it will recover now."

"Time heals many a great hurt, love." Sarah patted her daughter's hands and shook her head at the image before her. "Heaven knows it might have been worse."

Jocelyn nodded her agreement and looked to the distance when Tristan and Robin rode through the gate, both looking terribly drawn as they dismounted and passed their horses off to the waiting groom.

They'd spent the morning traveling the bounds of Summerly, coaxing the villagers out of hiding and sizing up what must be done to mend the damage.

"He seems a good man," Sarah observed, eyeing Tristan as he earnestly spoke with her husband.

"He is," Jocelyn answered, her heart faltering as she took in the sight of him.

Tristan was everything to her and so much more. In her angry foolishness, she nearly cast him aside.

"Your father told me all that is now Tristan's to bear and the burden is great. What will you do, Jocelyn?" Sarah asked, knowing her daughter's answer before she spoke it.

"Help him, if he will allow me to do so."

"It will never be easy. He has not only the debt of his father and a holding in shambles, but five sisters and an aunt to look after." Sarah felt her heart warm with her daughter's silence and nodded to herself.

Sarah knew her daughter better than to think she would abandon one whom she loved. Jocelyn had rushed to his aid after all, and at that time she'd been hurt and angry.

"It is good he will not be alone." Sarah kissed Jocelyn on the cheek and descended the stairs to join her husband.

Jocelyn watched her go, smiling to herself when her mother greeted Tristan warmly and sent him in her direction.

Tristan climbed the stairs, his eyes fixed on her, his mouth smoothed out in a line.

"Good morrow, sweet Lady. What do you standing here alone?" Tristan asked, taking hold of her hand to bring it to his lips.

"Awaiting your return. My mother tells me Bethany will make a full recovery," Jocelyn informed him.

They'd had very little time to speak once the fighting was through and Doyle was no longer a threat. Summerly needed looking after, those who were hurt needed to be tended and the damage assessed.

"I am glad to hear it." Tristan smoothed his hand through his hair and stood beside her, turning his eyes to the yard below.

Jocelyn watched him shake his head and heard the deep frustrated sigh escape his lips. She wished she had glad tidings to give him concerning the well-being of his keep, but she had none.

Bethany would heal in time and the horrid memories of yesterday would fade, but the destruction before them was another matter altogether.

There was nothing left in Summerly's coffers. There would be very little left to harvest in the fall and she feared Tristan's pride would prevent him from accepting her help.

"It is lost," Tristan whispered after a long moment of silence.

All that might have been his was gone. Were he to salvage it at all, it would indeed be a miracle.

The thick emotion in his voice caused her heart to ache for him. Jocelyn laced her fingers through his and blinked back her tears, forcing herself to find strength for this man.

"Come with me, Tristan." Jocelyn pulled him down the stairs and across the yard to the gate.

They slowly walked through the village, the smell of smoldering ash burning their nostrils as they passed the crumbling dwellings by.

When the village lanes ended and the fields were behind them, Jocelyn brought their walking to an end. They stood on the cliff line, looking out over the stretch of sea and the waves rolling in to crash against the shore below.

"Standing here, one might forget about the destruction that exists only a short distance away," Tristan remarked, his voice low and rough.

"Will you allow me to help you?" Jocelyn asked.

"Nay, Jocelyn, not in this. Summerly is my responsibility alone. I could not place such a burden on your shoulders." He shook his head with his determined words, his eyes remained fixed on the sea.

"I am more than capable of such a burden," she stated, squeezing his hand tightly, willing him to accept. "I would have conditions of my own for such help if that might assist in convincing you."

"This is not what you wanted, Jocelyn. This is precisely what you were struggling to avoid." Tristan gestured to the ruin behind them, his voice constricted with emotion.

"You deserve so much more than what I will bring you," Tristan muttered, bringing his attention back to the rolling waves below them.

"Nay, you are sorely mistaken," she whispered, reaching up to place her palm against his cheek, forcing him to look at her.

"You are everything to me. I care not that you bring into my life a keep that is crumbling, for it brought us together. Nor do I care that you bring with you five sisters, for I cherish them as my own and would suffer greatly if they were not a part of my life." Jocelyn swallowed her tears, struggling to tell him all her heart contained before she no longer had the voice to speak.

"I know, with the greatest of conviction, that you love me for the woman I am, for you told me yourself I am a ragbag urchin who dresses as a man. All I have ever wanted is to be loved for who I am."

Tristan tipped his head toward the heavens and took in a shaky breath that caused her to laugh in spite of herself.

"Would you not even ask to know my conditions for such assistance?" Jocelyn asked, causing him to look down at her once more.

For a moment, Tristan dared not ask for fear he could never own up to such conditions, but the smile on her lovely face urged to him wonder.

"Aye, sweet Lady. What conditions would you ask of me?" Tristan questioned, his adoration for her swelling his poor heart.

"Marry me, Tristan!" she yelled with a joyful laugh, tears coursing down her cheeks as she took hold of his shoulders. "For I am an heiress who is more than able to right all the wrongs life has committed against you."

Tristan looked down at her in wonder, shaking his head at her. His brow furrowed into a scowl when she continued to smile up at him as though her joy might truly bubble over.

"Nay, sweet Lady, you are the woman who has stolen my heart. I love you, Jocelyn. Were you nothing more than the ragged urchin I first thought you to be, I would love you as I do now." Tristan pulled her into his arms, holding her tightly feeling as though they would be consumed with joy.

"Then say aye, Tristan."

Jocelyn scowled at him when he pulled back and shook his head at her again.

He then fell to a knee before her, took hold of her hands and looked up at her with eyes littered with tears.

"Be my wife, Jocelyn?" Tristan asked, his voice low and rich in her ears.

"Aye," she answered with not so much as a breath of hesitation.

Jocelyn pulled on his hands, helping him to his feet and could not help but laugh when he took her face between his hands.

"I will cherish you, sweet Lady." Tristan bent and kissed her, sealing his vow with a tender kiss.

Chapter Seventeen

"Are you truly taking us with you to Artois?" Norissa exclaimed, bouncing up and down where she stood in the bustling yard.

"Hush Norissa," Millie chided, taking hold of her hand to quiet her sister's bouncing. "Why else would we be gathered in the yard at the break of day?"

"Release me, Millie. I was speaking to Jocelyn." Norissa pulled her hand free and tugged on the hem of Jocelyn's tunic. "Truly are we?"

"Aye, love," Jocelyn answered, unable to keep from smiling down at the little girl.

"All of us?" Anne questioned, clearly not wanting to be left behind.

"Aye, all of you," Tristan informed them, coming to stand beside Jocelyn.

He placed his hand on the small of her back and offered her an all-knowing smile when she looked up at him.

"Now into the carriage, it will be a tedious journey as it is, there is no reason to prolong it." He lifted Norissa and Anne up into the carriage then offered the three older girls his hand.

Tristan shook his head at his poor aunt when she grasped his offered hand and stepped up after her nieces.

"Are you sure you would rather not ride?" Tristan nearly laughed, knowing a fortnight on the road, confined to a carriage, with his sisters, would be unpleasant at best.

"Nay, I would have it no other way," Mona assured him, patting Tristan on the cheek before stepping fully into the carriage, instantly chastising Anne for tormenting her sister before she even had a chance to sit down.

"They are constant," Tristan laughed, taking hold of Jocelyn's hand to lead her across the short distance to where their mounts were waiting.

"Aye, constant and comforting," Jocelyn agreed, pausing beside her horse to study him carefully in the dim early morning light.

Near a month had passed since they'd won their freedom and in spite of the circumstances that brought them to this point in their lives, she could not help but feel as though this was how it was always meant to be.

After hours and hours of convincing, Tristan set aside his pride he and agreed to allow her to settle his father's debts and see to the full reconstruction of Summerly.

She was to be his wife, there was no reason why they should not begin to mend the past now so that they might move smoothly on to the future.

His father's holding would never be their home, but one day, when Bethany was older, it would be her inheritance. For now, it would remain under Tomas's watchful eye.

The village was in the process of being rebuilt and once they reached Artois, supplies would be sent back to Summerly to be certain the keep would last through the winter months.

Jocelyn was certain in only a matter of years, that which was once prosperous, would be so again.

"Are you certain?" Jocelyn asked one final time, gazing up into his eyes, knowing Tristan was not the sort of man to easily accept what she was offering him.

"There is nothing left for me here," he assured her. "My life is with you, sweet Lady." He bent and kissed her hands, looking at them for a moment as he contemplated what their life would be.

There was no doubt in his mind that he needed her, they all needed her.

Even if he sought to rebuild Summerly on his own, the place would be only a vacant reminder of what he might have had.

Without this amazing woman, he would be nothing. It mattered not where they went or how they passed their days, as long as they were together.

It was he who suggested they wait until they reached Artois to be wed. Tristan wanted nothing more than for the whole of her family to be present on the occasion.

Jocelyn's family were her life and Tristan was determined to begin their life together surrounded by those whom she loves.

His life at Summerly was in the past.

All that remained for him there was the constant reminder of how she was nearly taken from him. How he might have lost her and the destruction that was wrought.

He could not pass through the walls of the castle without remembering all that took place that horrid morning.

"You will not regret?" Jocelyn questioned, searching his face as she spoke.

"Never."

"Are you not going to kiss her?" Norissa called out from where she was leaning out the window of the carriage.

"Norissa," the other girls scolded, attempting to pull her back inside.

"Behave," Millie ordered, taking hold of her sister's gown, struggling to make Norissa come away from the window.

"Nay, I will not behave," Norissa stated, slapping at her sisters tugging hands.

"Kiss her Tristan, after all she is to be your wife," Norissa ordered, her voice filled with laughter when she was joined at the window by her siblings and even her beaming aunt.

"Perhaps it is you who will regret?" Tristan teased, taking hold of Jocelyn tenderly by the back of her neck.

"Nay," Jocelyn breathed just as he bent and claimed a kiss, causing an uproar of squeals and clapping from his sisters.

"I am helplessly smitten," Jocelyn confessed when he pulled back and glared in the direction of the disrespectful gaggle of little girls, causing them to duck back into the cover of the carriage.

"That is well, for I fear I am lost to you as well." He took hold of her about the waist and helped her up onto her waiting mount.

"Come, love of mine. Let us begin this journey."

Jocelyn nodded her agreement and put heel to her horse, smiling to herself as they passed through the gates of Summerly.

The crisp sea breeze kissed her cheeks, the gulls called out from the skies above them.

It was in that very moment, when Jocelyn turned to look into the pale green eyes of the man who would be her husband, that she realized all she had ever truly longed for was hers.

With this man by her side, she was whole.

The End

For more information on books
written by K.L. Brown go to
http://authorklbrown.blogspot.com

Made in the USA
San Bernardino, CA
05 July 2016